To ride
the gods' own
Stallion

A MELANIE KROUPA BOOK

To ride
the gods' own
Stallion

DIANE LEE WILSON

DK
Ink

DORLING KINDERSLEY PUBLISHING, INC.

A Melanie Kroupa Book

Dorling Kindersley Publishing, Inc.
95 Madison Avenue
New York, New York 10016

Visit us on the World Wide Web at http://www.dk.com

Dorling Kindersley books are available at special discounts for bulk purchases for sales
promotions or premiums. Special editions, including personalized covers, excerpts of
existing guides, and corporate imprints can be created in large quantities for specific
needs. For more information, contact Special Markets Dept., Dorling Kindersley
Publishing, Inc., 95 Madison Ave., New York, NY 10016; fax: (800) 600-9098.

Library of Congress Cataloging-in-Publication Data
Wilson, Diane L.
To ride the gods' own stallion / Diane Lee Wilson. — 1st ed.
p. cm.
"A Melanie Kroupa book."
Summary: After being taken as a slave to Nineveh, thirteen-year-old
Soulai finds his life intertwined with that of the son of King
Ashurbanipal and a magnificent stallion and gets a chance to prove to
himself and others that he is not a coward.
ISBN 0-7894-6802-6
[1. Slaves—Fiction. 2. Princes—Fiction. 3. Horses—Fiction. 4.
Nineveh (Extinct city)—Fiction.] I. Title.
PZ7. W69057 To 2000   [Fic]—dc21   00-031491

Book design by Jennifer Browne.
The text of this book is set in 11 point Trump Mediaeval.
Map by Susan Detrich

Printed and bound in U.S.A.

First Edition, 2000
2   4   6   8   10   9   7   5   3   1

Dedicated to my parents,

who gave me love and taught me confidence

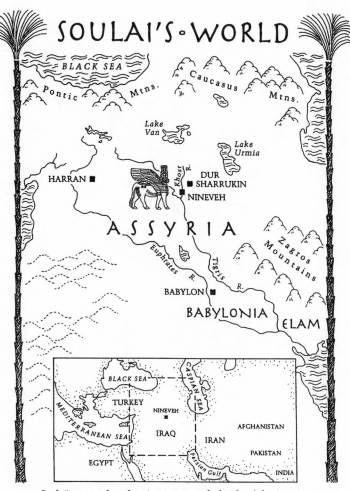

SOULAI'S WORLD

BLACK SEA

Pontic Mtns.

Caucasus Mtns.

Lake Van

Lake Urmia

HARRAN ■

Khosr R.

DUR SHARRUKIN ■

NINEVEH ■

A S S Y R I A

Zagros Mountains

Euphrates R.

Tigris R.

BABYLON ■

B A B Y L O N I A

ELAM

BLACK SEA

CASPIAN SEA

TURKEY

NINEVEH ■

AFGHANISTAN

MEDITERRANEAN SEA

IRAQ

IRAN

PAKISTAN

EGYPT

Persian Gulf

INDIA

Soulai's story takes place in 640 B.C., at the height of the Assyrian
Empire. In 612 B.C., some fifteen years after Ashurbanipal's death,
the city of Nineveh was conquered by the Medes and Babylonians.
The land surrounding that ancient city is now part of Iraq.

PART 1

Zagros foothills, Assyria, 640 B.C.

Only the gods saw the mottled yellow snake slip through the thatched roof. It had been two months since she had eaten and her flickering tongue sensed the warmth of life inside the mud-brick home. She stretched downward through the darkness, found safety in a pile of long reins, and coiled, waiting.

At first there was no movement. Then a delicious rustling pulled her forward. Slithering through a maze of yokes and cruppers, she came to a corner of the room that was lighter, and warmer. An oil lamp cast its wavery glow over a grouping of clay horses. She raised up and stared at the sculptures—this one fixed in a voiceless whinny, that one in a suspended prance—and knew something among them was moving. She tasted the air. And lunged!

At the same instant that a rat quivered in her jaws,

the lamp tipped and fell. Fire splashed across her back, sending her up the mud wall.

She wanted to rest, to wrap her coils around the rat and squeeze the life from it, but the heat was following her. Singed scales began to burn anew as rising flames licked at the dried thatch. Clenching her jaws, she glided to the ground, disappearing into the night just as the fire burst through the roof.

DUST AND ASHES

Better that you'd never been born.

The words still burned in Soulai's ears. He hugged his knees and rocked back and forth. The other villagers joined in the evening's ceremonial wailing, but Soulai's throat was too dry to cry anymore.

For thirteen years he'd sat around the fire with everyone else on this first night of the month of Tammuz and mourned Nature's death. He knew that while the goddess made her summer-long journey through the underworld, his mountain would wither and die. Leaves were already starting to fall from parched tree limbs, in fact, and this day had certainly been the hottest of the year.

But tonight Soulai was mourning his own death. *Better that you'd never been born*, his father had said. They hadn't shared a word or glance since, and Soulai had begun to feel that his existence, in his father's eyes, had ended.

Blinking back tears, he picked up the ball of damp clay at his side and tossed it into the air. With each smacking return to his hands, he punished himself. You should have been watching the bushes, he scolded. You should have readied a pile of rocks. When the lion attacked you should have . . .

The clay hit the ground with a thud. Quickly he picked it up and brushed away the dirt. He felt a shiver of fear. He knew what he *should* have done, but he'd searched to the core of his being and hadn't found the bravery. It just wasn't there.

Stroking the gritty weight with one thumb, he looked up at the sky. The brilliant constellations that normally came to life before his eyes seemed to hover at a distance. There was the magnificent scorpion, poised just above the southern horizon, its glittering tail curled over its back like a giant fishhook. At its center, the one star that usually flared from copper to red to gold shone without a flicker. And the serpent handler, who endlessly struggled to contain the giant snake, wasn't moving at all. Soulai had a dizzying sensation that the world was pulling away from him. Maybe I'm dead already, he thought.

"Soulai!"

He jumped. But it was only his older sister, Soulassa. He tossed his ball of clay into the air again.

"He'll see you," she warned. "He's with Uncle in the hut right behind you."

"He's drunk by now."

"He's not blind."

Bitterness engulfed him. "He might as well be. He doesn't see *me.*"

"Soulai." The voice was still chiding, though gentler. "If you'd look up from your clay once in a while, you'd see things better. Such as lions. You were fooling with it today, weren't you—your clay?"

Why not ask if I'd been breathing today? Soulai thought. As if I had some choice in reaching for the stuff each morning. As if I could stop my fingers from digging to find the form that lies hidden inside each lump. It was so much easier to hide in his clay, easier than facing life. Or death.

"You're getting too old for this," his sister went on. "I'm not going to be around much longer to protect you—I'm getting married, remember? Who's going to chase away your lions then?"

The question went unanswered; Soulai hunched his shoulders and started slapping the ball of clay from palm to palm. When he did lift his head, Soulassa was gone.

"In a village not very far from this one," the storyteller began, "there once lived a lazy man."

The ritual was complete. The men from this, his

7

uncle's village, and from nearby villages, now sprawled around the embers, bellies aching from the longest-day feast and the celebration of his sister's impending marriage. Their shoulders sagged as they fell under the magic of the soothing words. Children dozed in the laps of their mothers and sisters, who rocked back and forth in unconscious rhythm. Boys like Soulai who had grown past rocking slipped off into the silver-lit forest for their own celebrating.

Embarrassment over the day's events, and misery over his father's words, kept Soulai from joining them. They were all champing at the bit to become men. But he? He'd resigned himself to the role of coward, running to his clay each time he stumbled into trouble.

With a heavy sigh, he set to squeezing the clay into shape. Then, remembering Soulassa's warning, he hid it in his lap and glanced over his shoulder. His father and mother, along with his two younger sisters and an infant brother, remained in the hut behind him. So he flipped the clay into the air and pressed it between his palms again. Still thinking, he began molding it.

He'd tried to shape himself into the sort of son his father wanted. He'd sat at his father's side and attempted to learn the skills of the harness-maker. But where only a strap was needed, he'd found it necessary to add a decorative fringe. And a breast-collar couldn't leave his hands without some intricate pattern tooled into it. With great pride, he'd shown his work to his father. "You're wasting your time," his father had growled. "An ass can't look in a mirror."

Soulai studied the clay in his hands and frowned. For some reason it wasn't responding tonight. He bit his lip. There was also a nagging feeling that he had forgotten something. He shook his head, collapsed the lump between his hands, and started over.

After his failure as a harness-maker—at least in his father's eyes—he'd been banished to the hills as a goatherd. But even at this simplest of tasks, Soulai had disgraced himself—that very afternoon, in fact, when he hadn't seen the lion's approach. It had pounced so suddenly, bloodying one goat and killing another. Soulassa had appeared just as quickly, screaming at the top of her lungs. Her shouts had easily drowned his own cry, as he had scrambled behind a pistachio tree. Through its branches he'd marveled at how bravely his sister had run up to the startled creature, at how her wool tunic had strained across the muscles of her broad shoulders as she'd heaved clumps of dirt and sticks at it. And the lion had actually run away!

He shook his head again. My own sister . . . more of a man than me. She and her betrothed will marry and have many children, no doubt all strong boned and brave like her. Maybe they'll even name one after me. The smile melted from his face. What kind of fate would that be, to be named after a person so worthless that his own father would wish he'd never been born?

"And then I shall move to a big house in a big city, and I shall . . ."

The storyteller's words faded away as Soulai clenched his teeth and pummeled the clay with his fist. He slapped it loudly between his hands, then bent over it and worked furiously. Black curls fell across his lean cheeks. His breathing quickened. An unseen fire crept through his fingers, and, as if by the gods' own hands, a lifelike creature began to arise from the clay.

While animals of all kinds leaped from his fingers, horses were his favorite subject and a small herd of them lay hidden in the corner of his thatched-roof hut. He had taken them out this evening, in fact, after his family had left for his uncle's village, and he had admired them by the flame of the oil lamp. Soulassa's words returned to him and he blushed. Of course he was too old to actually play with them. But they still came to life in his dreams, and he could choose to hitch his chariot to a pair of powerful, feather-crowned chargers or throw a leg over the back of a restive stallion and gallop beneath starlit skies across the Assyrian flatlands. It was the only time he was truly happy.

He coaxed an arching neck from the clay and pinched a windblown mane along its ridge, then, dissatisfied, smashed the features and began again. Horses were the hardest to bring to life, for his village owned none, only a few donkeys. Trying to fashion this creature of the gods when he had only its long-eared, hairy-hided cousins for models frustrated him. But the trader Jahdunlim had a horse, and he might be climbing the trail to the village tomorrow. Soulai looked forward to watching the animal on its tether; he'd remember to note the shift of balance when it pawed the ground, the angles of the small ears cocked this way and that, and the exact arc of the head and neck as the horse reached around to nip at a fly. For weeks after Jahdunlim had come and gone, Soulai knew he'd sculpt in a frenzy.

There was one time when the trader had spied some of Soulai's creations, scooped them up—though none of the horses, Soulai wouldn't allow it—and carried them down the mountain. Months later, he had returned with a copper piece for Soulai. His father had hurrahed and wanted to trade it right back to Jahdunlim, who, with a greedy eye, just happened to have brought with him a new awl and a handful of needles. But Soulai had refused. The animals he had birthed were his and he would keep the offered compensation for their loss.

For a whole day he clutched the copper, squeezing

nail marks into his palm for fear he would lose it. He savored its hammered hardness and smelled the tangy odor mingling with his sweat. The next day he had punched a hole in it, pierced it with a thong, and draped it around his neck.

At the time he'd thought he would keep it forever, but now he intended to give it to Soulassa to add to her meager dowry. He was ready, even, to trade some of his beloved horses to Jahdunlim. This he would do for his sister, the one who always outshone him, but the only one who tried to understand him.

Soulai lifted a hand and fingered the metal piece now. He again looked up at the scorpion in the sky, at its lovely copper-colored star. There was something unusual about the way it was glowing, brighter and brighter. Other stars seemed to unstick themselves from the sky and float with it. Then more and more, brilliant bits of fire that . . .

"Fire! Fire!"

The first shouts flew past Soulai's ears. He thought they were part of the story.

"Soulai!" Some boys came running into the circle, out of breath. "We can see your house burning! Where's your father?"

Before he could answer, his father bolted from his

brother's hut. He wiped his hands on his tunic and, at the last instant, leaped over his son kneeling in the dirt. "How bad?" Soulai heard his father ask as they raced down the mountainside through the darkness. He heard no answer. But a thick drift of smoke suddenly wrinkled his nostrils. With his next heartbeat he was sprinting after them, vaguely aware that his mother was already moaning and gathering the youngsters into her arms.

Luminous orange sparks were bursting into the black sky ahead of him. By the time he'd careered down the winding footpath, jumped the stream, and entered the small clearing that separated their home from the others in the village, Soulai saw that it was fully ablaze. The walls pulsated red; the thatched roof—what wasn't floating away as weightless cinders—shivered in an ocean of ripping flames.

He felt his stomach tighten. The lamp—did I leave it burning? Is the fire *my* fault?

"Oh, Soulai." His sister's fingers wrapped around his arm. The pity in her voice made him wonder if she knew. "Your horses." The remains of the crackling roof collapsed with a loud crash, burying his creations along with the sound of her words.

Tears stung his eyes. He truly was worthless! His

father was right; he should never have been born. Fearfully, he glanced over at his father, standing among the awestruck villagers. The orange glow couldn't hide the fact that his face had gone pale. But it took another loud snap and spray of sparks to bring the real horror to Soulai's attention.

With his stomach doubled in a painful knot, he looked back into the flames: Jahdunlim's tack! Every last bit of it was crumbling to ash: twin sets of fine harness, splendidly supple driving reins, and several silver-studded bridles, all repaired by Soulai's father and awaiting the trader's return. There was a whip, too, or there had been; a knob-handled one with a long tail that Soulai had helped rebraid into three clawlike tassels. Oxen would never again suffer its sting, Soulai thought, but Jahdunlim owned many more whips . . . and a fiercer temper than his father. His mind spun. For the first time, horse or no, he dreaded Jahdunlim's coming.

IN THE SERPENT'S COILS

"I'm begging you for more time, Jahdunlim. Only some more time."

Soulai's shoulders tensed at the sound of his father's pleading. Exhausted from the long night, and strangled by guilt, he squatted in the corner of their burned-out home and pretended to study one of his few undamaged horse figurines. He turned it over and over in his hands. The clay body, newly hardened, was still warm from the fire. It seemed almost alive.

"And what would you do with more time?" Jahdunlim snapped, as he stood outside the charred door frame. He refused to set foot in the remains of their home. Soulai's mother, hurt by this dishonor, pursed her lips. She swept the ashes into random piles, then absently restacked fallen mud bricks. "Time cannot birth new harness," the trader barked. "Time cannot mold new silver."

Soulai's father humbly spread his palms. "Only in time can I replace your valuables. I promise I will make you new harness, new reins—"

"There is no time for promises, man," Jahdunlim interrupted. "This is business. Now. Promises pay no silver." He cursed and clapped the butt of his stubby whip across his palm. Soulai glanced up. To his surprise, the man's piercing black eyes were appraising him.

Jahdunlim abruptly turned away. "Follow," he ordered, and Soulai's father obediently trailed the trader away from the wreckage, all the way to the curve in the mountain footpath.

Jahdunlim's horse, tied to a small wild pear tree, nickered, and Soulai shifted his gaze. The skinny gelding was a different one from the last visit. His mane hung dirty and matted, and flies swarmed around his weepy eyes. As unkempt as the horse was, however, the rug and bridle could not have been more handsome. Jahdunlim has an eye for fine things, Soulai thought. He turned back to watch the two men. Their vehement gestures showed that the talking had turned quickly to arguing.

Guilt stabbed him again. Every bit of this is my fault, he grieved, my second disaster in two days. And all because of the clay. Was it worth it?

Unconsciously he stroked the figurine cradled in his

hand. It had been one of his favorites: a long-maned stallion, head thrust into the wind, nostrils flared. The fire had forged hairline cracks in the neck and loin, but otherwise the horse had emerged looking the same. Still, it felt different. He rubbed some soot from the haunches and tapped the horse's barrel. It clanked. Carefully he set it in the ashes at the end of a row of rearing and prancing figurines, some now headless, some three-legged.

"Soulai!" his mother whispered at his shoulder. "You stay here. I'm going to get your sisters and the baby. Your uncle, too." She shot a glance at Jahdunlim, who was at that moment jabbing her husband in the chest. "And you watch that one," she warned. "Worse than the jackal he is, grabbing every last scrap for himself." She folded her arms and shivered, then hurried up the path.

The men stopped talking as Soulai's mother passed. The moment she was out of sight, however, Jahdunlim leaned close and shouted, "Choose!"

Soulai saw his father shrink. An uncharacteristic expression distorted his face. Slowly he turned, head down, and walked toward the blackened skeleton of their home and workplace. Jahdunlim skulked in his shadow, eyes fixed upon Soulai. When the men stood before him, he forced his trembling legs to stand. His father had a queer look in his eyes.

17

"I'm sorry, Soulai," he said. "There is no other way." His leathery hands roughly gripped Soulai's wrists. From somewhere Jahdunlim produced a thong that he wrapped around them, pulling the knot so tight that it bit into the skin. Soulai gasped and jerked away. But the thong held snug. Panicked, he glanced from his bound wrists to his father's stony face and then to Jahdunlim's yellow grin. With a sudden chill, he knew the price of his weakness.

"No more than five years," his father stated, the slight tone of uncertainty multiplying Soulai's fears.

The trader threw back his head and laughed. "Are you saying you don't trust me? The word of Jahdunlim is known from Harran to Babylon. Now, I'm off. I have customers waiting."

Footsteps sounded and Soulai looked up to see Soulassa sprinting down the path ahead of several villagers. His mother hurried along, the baby clamped to her chest with one arm and his youngest sister balanced on her hip with the other. An aunt, clutching the hand of another sister, bustled alongside his uncle. Tagging behind, exchanging inquisitive looks, came two boys his own age. There were others, he knew, but Soulai's vision suddenly blurred. He managed to swallow the cry that shot to his lips, only to hear it burst from his mother's.

"He comes of free will," Jahdunlim shouted. He lifted

his whip as a weapon and halted everyone except Soulai's mother. She slid her daughter from her hip and, wailing brokenheartedly, rushed to embrace her son. The baby's high-pitched voice joined in.

"Why? Why? Why?" she cried, first to the sky, then to her husband.

Scowling, he yanked her free. "It's the only way," he repeated. "I had to choose one of the children. And he's the one who . . ." His hasty glance at Soulai revealed his disappointment. Gathering his composure, he straightened. "A man measures his worth in his scars," he said gruffly. "In five years your son will come back a man."

At the mention of five years Soulai's mother ceased her crying. She took a wavering step backward and her free hand hovered near the empty O of her mouth. The jaws of his two friends fell open and their eyes met Soulai's. Crushing humiliation made him look away. Standing apart from everyone was Soulassa. Her black eyes darted from her brother to her father, then back again.

The baby's crying rose a pitch and Soulai fought against bursting into tears himself. He ached to feel his mother's arms enfold him. I'm not ready to be a man, he wanted to scream, not yet! I'm just a boy—a smallish, bony-shouldered boy who runs from lions. Can't you all see that?

But Jahdunlim was prodding him toward the path leading from the village. The trader tore free the reins of his gelding. Instead of mounting, however, he used the animal and himself as buffers for their retreat. Soulai glanced over his shoulder. The image he carried with him was of his mother kneeling upon the ground, one trembling hand covering her mouth; of his father, stiff-jawed and silent; and of Soulassa, calmly gathering his horse sculptures into her arms.

It seemed fitting, he thought, that since he had mourned his death last night, he'd have a funeral procession today. His life was over. He wasn't a man; he wasn't even a son. He was merely a thing to be bartered.

Head bowed, he stumbled down the dirt path. The thong cut into his skin with each step, inscribing his father's words: *A man measures his worth in his scars.* That thought brought prickles of sweat to his body. His legs grew shaky, and he slowed his steps for fear that just stubbing a toe might fling him over the mountain-side—though actual death, he considered for a grim instant, would be just. Because I should never have been born.

While he had never traveled from the mountains surrounding his village, Soulai knew from his father's stories where this path led. Two more hillocks ahead, and after a big loop to the left, they would come upon a huge stone aqueduct—the width of four men laid end to end—that sucked water from a spring. Like a giant snake it stretched all the way down the mountain, disappearing in the shimmering heat of the flatlands. He'd been told that the stone serpent's body stretched two days' journey on foot to Nineveh, royal seat of the Assyrian kingdom—a city populated with thousands of men . . . and their slaves. According to his father, it was a city of such cruelty that one misstep could leave you impaled, still breathing, eyes bulging, upon the city gates. His heart pounded against his thin chest as he struggled for breath. His sight blurred again and this time he let the tears come. This had to be an awful dream. Sick to his stomach and swaying on his feet, Soulai halted, trying to shake away the horrible images.

A sharp pain stabbed his buttocks as Jahdunlim swatted his whip handle across them once, then twice. "Move along," the man growled. Soulai's vision cleared. Sweat continued trickling down his wrists, burning salt into his chafing wounds, and he knew he would not awaken from this nightmare.

ONE OF 3 MANY

The underworld. The shadowy realm of the dead. This has to be it, Soulai thought as he shifted uncomfortably upon his mat. "This has to be the underworld," he murmured.

"Welcome to it," came a drowsy voice from the other side of the room. "Will you keep to silence?" came another. Soulai flushed. He had thought them all asleep. Now, as a cockroach grabbled its way across the low ceiling of the cramped room, he was grateful for the early morning darkness.

Tired as he was, he'd once again barely slept. Only a few weeks of slavery had passed, and the five years of bondage still looming in front of him weighed on him. Miserably he poked with his foot at a flake of plaster until it fell away with a faint tinkling sound. Sticking his toe into the hollow, he sensed a slight bit of moisture. It reminded him of his clay. How long it seemed since he'd cradled a damp ball of the stuff in his hands and anticipated its possibilities. No possibilities existed now: The mud and clay that surrounded him were dried up and crumbling.

Like I am, he thought, as his fingers touched the small tag attached to the choking thong around his neck. It had replaced his precious copper coin, which Jahdunlim had snatched back as "owed to him." Wedge-shaped symbols had been scratched, then baked, into the clay surface of the tag. He couldn't read the marks, but he'd been told that they spoke his own name, as well as that of one of King Ashurbanipal's sons— Habasle, a man he had yet to meet, a man who now, oddly enough, owned him.

For the hundredth agonizing time, Soulai recalled how Jahdunlim had marched him two long and dusty days toward Nineveh where, on the third day, in a bustling marketplace crowded with oxen, goats, donkeys, and hinnies, he'd traded him and some sheep for a few pieces of silver. Led away to the palace by a stranger, Soulai had been shoved into a line of other men and boys. He'd been touched and poked. His tongue had been yanked nearly out of his mouth, his hair chopped off above his ears. And then he'd been branded. Never in his life had he known such searing pain.

The star-shaped wound on his left shoulder burned

afresh at the memory, and he winced as the scabbed outline caught on the hairs of the palace's itchy wool tunic. Between the sores on his wrists and the one on his back, he was collecting scars, all right. Am I a man yet? he wanted to cry out to his father.

"It's too hard," he groaned instead.

An annoyed sigh preceded the rise of one of the room's occupants. The boy, or man—it was hard to tell—swung to a sitting position and carefully lit the smoky oil lamp that served as their only amenity. Lifting it high, he leveled an impassive gaze at Soulai. An ugly, pinkish scar stretched from his hairline across an empty eye socket and past his cheekbone. "Whining won't help."

"I wasn't whining," Soulai retorted, knowing he lied. He climbed to his feet, barely able to straighten in the little room. Although sunshine had yet to poke beneath the flimsy wooden door, he could already hear hundreds of sandaled feet marching across dusty tiles. Another day's labor as a slave was dawning.

"It's just that . . . that . . . "—he was struggling for words, sounding dangerously childish—". . . five years of my life seems—"

"Your life?" the lampholder interrupted. "Your life matters not a lick. In fact, you don't even exist." He snorted in disdain. "Look around you, boy. You're one of us now—no more than a shadow, no more important than dust."

The grim fortune, told so bluntly, stunned Soulai into silence. He felt as if hands were tightening around his throat. Rushing for the door, he shoved it open and ran out.

But the dark morning offered little relief; the air already hung heavy with the threat of coming heat, and red-mouthed hearths belched as much smoke as bread. He bit his lip. Ducking between a parade of platters piled high with oily dates and rosy pomegranates, he stared with renewed horror at the snaking line of placid-faced servants. One after another they came, as silent and lifeless as shadows. His fists tightened. No! He couldn't be so easily harnessed. But in his next step, one of the rigid sandals he'd been forced to strap onto his feet caught in a crack and he tumbled headlong onto the courtyard tiles. Climbing to his knees, he found himself staring into one of a dozen reed birdcages stacked beneath an alabaster colonnade. A broken-feathered creature that had once shimmered with the colors of the rainbow lay on its side, beak slightly agape, dead.

Soulai felt his own mouth fall open, felt the same struggle for breath. Panic was beginning to take a strong hold on him when the hungry whinnies of horses broke the morning air. Ti would be waiting, he thought. The one unquenchable flame in this gray world. For Ti, he could hurry.

Rising, he ran across the small courtyard, dashed down another flight of stairs, and sank into the musky aroma of the royal stables. Lanterns lined the brick walls, dispersing their yellow glow up to the thatched roof. The lights were reflected in the dark eyes of a thousand restless horses tethered side by side in long rows. Other stable boys like Soulai were arriving, picking up the rush-woven baskets stacked beside the doorway and sleepily heading off to the grain master to receive their allotment.

Ten of the royal horses—three geldings, two colts, and five stallions—were assigned to Soulai's care. In all his life, he'd never seen animals as beautiful as these. His fingers trembled just to touch them. With their chiseled heads and large, liquid eyes, these creatures were as different from the mounts that had passed through his village as peacocks were from pigeons.

They were looking for him now, "his" horses were, heads straining against their tethers. A shiver of awe, mixed with a little fear, ran the length of his body as he approached them. Half-hiding the full basket beneath his arm, he slipped in beside the first colt, a chestnut, and cupped a hand beneath the bony jowl. The colt dove for the grain, but Soulai used his own head to block the way. He guided the horse's muzzle to his face until nostril touched nostril. Slowly he exhaled his greeting. The animal responded by standing stone still and taking in the scent. Then his wide nostrils fluttered as he blew back a greeting of his own. The magic lasted only an instant. In the next breath the horse tossed his head and nickered impatiently for his grain. Soulai scooped two handfuls into the stone trough that ran the length of the stable and grinned as the soft muzzle tore into it. As he walked around the chestnut to the next horse, he carefully ran his eye over the animal's body, checking for any cuts or swellings that could mar perfection.

In this manner he worked his way from one horse to the next, petting, feeding, appraising. His heart began to beat faster as he fed the seventh and eighth horses. But he forced himself to take smaller and slower steps. He fed the ninth, taking the time to tentatively rub the broad forehead and watch the grain dribble through his fingers into the trough. Only then did Soulai lift his eyes.

His throat caught. The tenth horse, a young stallion named Ti, was staring at him. Staring right through him, really, as though he didn't exist. But, as always, Soulai was mesmerized. The horse embodied everything he had ever tried to mold from clay: flightiness blended with fieriness, graceful beauty disguising explosive power. When Ti swelled his neck and shook his mane and split the air with his defiant whistle, Soulai was filled with such awe that in that moment he could almost forget his own slavery.

Ti. The name was Sumerian, meaning *arrow* or *life*. He, too, was new to the stable, having just been purchased from the famed horse breeders of Lake Urmia. Three years of age, Soulai had been told, and, while the stallion accepted a rider on his back, he had yet to learn to pull a chariot or to stand quietly while the arrow was let loose—though he could certainly gallop as swiftly as the arrow's flight. Soulai remembered with a grimace how on his first day at the palace, on the way to the drinking trough in the crowded stable courtyard, Ti had pulled the lead rope from his inexperienced hands. To Soulai's churning mix of embarrassment and admiration, Ti had careered around and around the walled enclosure, diabolically evading all outthrust arms. The excited horse had even challenged an older stallion, and a stouter one at that, by rearing up and striking at him with his hooves. When Soulai had finally managed to snatch the dangling lead, Ti had halted immediately. Then Ti had trumpeted his triumph to the hills. No one would question *his* bravery!

A nearby lamp cast flickering light across Ti's croup as Soulai moved alongside him. Even dimmed by the stable's smoky atmosphere, his sleek coat shone. Soulai ran his hand along the taut flank, the muscled shoulder and back, remembering with a smile how Ti had attracted all eyes on that first day. Splashed with large patches of both silver and gold, the stallion fairly shouted the promise of good fortune to anyone skilled enough to ride him. His silky mane and tail waved in a fitful breeze; his nostrils flared so wide as to show crimson in the light. But it was the horse's eyes that enchanted: one a milky blue that echoed the sky's endless depths, the other a gleaming yellow that challenged the sun's radiance.

The head charioteer to King Ashurbanipal had strode across the yard and chastised Soulai after he'd regained the lead rope. "You'll be duly warned to keep two eyes and two hands on the lead to this one," he had scolded. "Do you know?"

"Know?"

"What you have here?"

Intimidated by both the man and the horse, he'd shaken his head.

"A parti-color," the man snapped, and Soulai felt as ignorant as a small child. "A parti-color stallion fed on the grasses of Lake Urmia. And this bit of braided leather is all that's harnessing his power."

Soulai nodded uncertainly.

The charioteer cast an exasperated look heavenward,

then continued in a clipped tone. "Parti-color horses—especially those with odd eyes"—he was grasping the halter with both hands now and studying Ti's face—"are prized for their rarity and their bravery. You'll find no horse more ready for the hunt, boy. With some training, not even the roar of a lion will frighten one such as this." He placed his hands behind Ti's withers and leaned his weight on them. "Well-knit," he said, nodding. Then he slid an expert hand along Ti's shoulder and down his near foreleg. "Clean bones, sloping pastern." He traced his hand lightly up the leg and, stepping back, whistled in surprise. "Look here!" His fingers reverently outlined a large white patch upon Ti's shoulder. "It's a bird of some sort . . . a hawk, I think. Why, Ninurta, god of the hunt himself, has branded this colt with his own image." The man let out another low whistle and shook his head in admiration. The look changed to worry when it returned to Soulai. "You take care of this one, boy," he admonished, clapping Soulai sharply on the back. "The gods have important plans for him."

The memory of the charioteer's magical words had lulled Soulai into a trance. It took the sharp crack of Ti's hoof striking the stone trough to jolt him back to his chores. The stallion's ears were pinned back and he was tossing his head with growing anger. Soulai quickly scooped out two handfuls of grain and then added a third that he'd managed to skim from the rations of the other horses. He didn't dare push his nose-to-nose greeting on Ti. He had tried only once and been punished with a stinging, bare-toothed snap. Gingerly he touched the bruises on his cheekbone and longed more strongly than ever to befriend this stallion.

Ti continued to ignore him, however. So while the horse ate, Soulai skimmed his fingers along the sleek hide and down the left shoulder. Slowly he traced the image of the bird with outstretched wings. He could almost smell the crisp mountain air, could almost feel the hawk's wild freedom. A shiver of excitement rippled through him. The gods had plans for Ti. Maybe if I bind myself to him, he thought, an animal so brave that he can't be frightened even by a lion, maybe I can share his fate. That was it! Astride a stallion such as Ti, he'd escape this underworld; he'd find some way to prove that it was better he *had* been born.

HORSES AND MASTERS

"Lazy sons of a skinny she-bitch, all of you! Light a fire under your worthless feet before I grind you into dog meal!" The thundering command made Soulai jump. "There's an oxload of barley to be carried in, a mountain of manure to be carried out, and Shamash already shows his face in the sky."

Like a hundred other boys, Soulai scurried. Darting round a corner post, he unexpectedly stumbled face first into the royal stable master, Mousidnou, who had stopped his bellowing long enough to bite into an orange. Juice and seeds trickled through his long beard, and, as Soulai pulled himself away, a stickiness clung to his skin. He backed one cautious step, ducked his head respectfully, and tried to pick a careful path around the man's protruding belly. Before he could escape, however, a bear-sized paw of a hand smacked his buttocks.

"Pick up your ass and move it, boy! You want to wiggle it like that, I'll send you to dance in the harem."

A group of stable boys nearby snickered. Soulai flushed as he trotted on toward the hay storage. There, shoulder to shoulder, he fought his way to the front, absently counting the rhythmic pings and rushing sighs as the great sheaves of barley hay were slashed open to spill over the floor. He gathered an armload and staggered back to his horses, returned for another load, and then another. Afterward, he swept the aisle and offered to Ti what scraps of hay he'd gathered. The stallion accepted the morsel but ignored the affectionate pat accompanying it. Disappointed, Soulai tackled the watering.

Each of the royal horses was led to water three times daily and the noise exceeded even that of the feeding. Shrill whinnies split the air and hundreds of hooves clattered on brick as Soulai tentatively joined the procession. The excited horses could be dangerous. As if to remind him, the gray colt he was leading suddenly reared and a sharp hoof narrowly missed his head. Soulai snapped the lead rope, as he had seen other stable boys do, shouted, and shoved his own small weight against the fractious animal, finally managing to guide him to the courtyard.

When they'd both made it safely to the watering

trough, Soulai breathed a sigh of relief. This was his one opportunity to stand, without fear, and look around, for Mousidnou stressed that the horses must always be allowed to drink their fill.

The daily commotion of the palace was taking place along the tiered courtyards above his head. As on previous mornings, he noted that the bustle increased with the sun's ascent. He observed the long-robed scribes furiously carving messages onto clay tablets and palace servants sprinting with their missives. He saw the coded nods between passing guards who gripped cumbersome bows, the fringed parasols shielding royal heads while swaying palm fronds chased away flies. He wondered if one of those royal heads was that of his owner. But as three weeks had passed and he had yet to see the prince, Soulai had decided that the man must have no interest at all in horses.

When Ti's turn came, Soulai proudly led him to the end of the trough closest to the well. The water was coolest here, he reasoned, as he watched bucket after bucket rise from the dark mouth. This was another of his gifts to Ti, and he smiled as the stallion stretched out his neck and sucked noisily. He waited until the head was lifted, water dribbling from the fleshy lips, to search the jeweled eyes for acknowledgment. But Ti stood regal and expectant, looking right through him, as though he didn't exist.

Heaving a sigh, Soulai returned to the stable and the task of removing manure. Each morning he had to lug unwieldy basketfuls of warm green turds down the long aisle and out to an enclosure to be overturned onto mountainous heaps. There, slaves no older than one of his younger sisters worked all day raking the dung into a fine layer that baked in the sun. With his empty basket flopping against his calf, he shuffled around the moist clumps to another pile, this one brown and fluffy. He scooped the dried manure into his basket, then returned to the stable to sprinkle it atop the layer already packed down by hooves. He could see that lying in the powdered manure was good for the horses: Their coats gleamed as if polished with silk scarves.

"You, you, and you!" Mousidnou was coming through the stable again, bellowing his orders laced with threats. "Set rugs upon these three and trot them out to the armory. Now! And you'll fasten the girths tight or I'll use your scrawny sinews in their place." This sent Soulai sprinting, along with the other boys who had been singled out, to the stern-faced keeper of the royal tack. Begrudgingly the man handed out the required bridles and rugs. His yellowed eyes narrowed as he doled out his own threat to Soulai: Return them un-damaged or replace them with your own hide. Soulai swallowed hard and nodded.

It was the chestnut who had been chosen this time, and as soon as Soulai had him ready, he led the bit-champing horse out of the stable and out through the palace gates. A wide, curving ramp dropped them into the midst of the bustling city. Soulai's pulse quickened. A stench of rotting meat and urine-soaked straw choked this route to the armory, for it was flanked by Nineveh's zoo. Past the high walls he caught glimpses of the strangest animals: bulging-eyed birds standing twice as tall as him, white-faced monkeys reaching toward him with their almost human fingers, creatures with black twisted horns or curving yellow fangs. The strange howls and grunts made the back of his neck tingle. But there was one sound he dreaded more than any other, and he shuddered each time he heard it: the unmistak-able thunder of a lion. Once, he saw a thick-maned lion being hauled forth in a paneled wooden crate so small that the creature had to crouch. It took four strong men leaning into ropes to drag the snarling lion away. Soulai wondered about the animal's fate.

The instant the chestnut was delivered to the armory, Soulai raced back to the stable. Mousidnou was in full swing, barking out more orders. As fast as he could,

Soulai tacked up another horse and returned to the armory. By the time Shamash blazed high in the sky, Soulai was still bridling and unbridling and leading sweat-soaked, blowing horses to the watering trough.

The order for Ti to be readied came late in the day, and, as Soulai bent over to fasten the girth, the muscles in his back clenched with pain. To make matters worse, Ti bit him. Soulai jumped aside with a cry. Rubbing the welt, he looked tearfully at the gold and silver stallion. It was the insult, more than the injury, that hurt. He'd placed all his hopes in the horse, done everything he could to befriend him. But after three weeks, what was the use?

That night, curled on his mat, Soulai counted in small groans the bruises and cuts that another day's labors had branded into him. As usual, his thoughts wandered to Ti. He shut them off. The horse's indifference cut him more painfully than did any of his visible injuries.

Reaching for a happier time, he tried to recall the different horses he had sculpted from clay. But he couldn't picture any of them. He opened his eyes to the darkness and touched the tips of his fingers together. There had been a creative fire there once, he was sure of it. He had been able to pick up a lump of clay and create life from it. Now there was nothing.

When the next day dawned, Soulai climbed to his feet more lifeless than ever. He plodded through the routine, fell onto his mat at night, and began the next day in the same way. And then the one after that and the one after that. The days of his slavery became linked in an endless chain of dust and sun and sweat.

Until one hot morning in the month of Ab. He had completed the graining and, as usual, was lingering beside Ti. He never heard them coming; he saw Ti jerk his head up in alarm and in the next instant found himself backed against the trough. Two mastiffs, one liver-colored, one silver, were suddenly probing Soulai's body with their dripping noses. Ti shook his head in annoyance, then returned to eating. Soulai shrank back and held his breath.

"You!" An unfamiliar voice pulled his attention away from the dogs. Still clutching onto the stone trough, he looked up to see a smooth-skinned boy about his own age draped in a long, richly embroidered blue-and-white tunic. The boy pointed a finger at him. "Set a rug on this horse here and another on one for yourself." When he turned to speak to two men carrying bows, the mastiffs abandoned Soulai to romp in the aisle.

Soulai exhaled. He shook his head to clear the dizziness. Ready two horses? It was too early for training at the armory and, well, *he* was supposed to ride? He'd have to speak up. "The horses," he began, "they haven't had their hay. And they need water."

The boy spun, the silky fringe on his tunic swirling about his ankles. He appeared to grow taller at will. "Who are you to speak thus to me?"

A small alarm sounded in Soulai's head.

"Answer me!"

"I'm Soulai," he responded in a voice suddenly so parched it crackled to a whisper. "I care for these ten horses." He stiffly extended his arm to indicate the well-groomed animals busily nibbling their last bits of grain. "They still need hay and water."

The boy stepped close to Soulai, causing the mastiffs to swing their attention back to him. One shoved his nose up under Soulai's short tunic, sniffing between his legs. He pushed at the dog's massive head with both hands; a sick fear told him he was about to be bloodied. To add to his torment, the fancily dressed boy was sharply tapping the clay tag resting on Soulai's chest. A hammered silver bracelet set with lavender stones shimmered on his forearm. An intricately carved blue stone hung from his neck. These, and the overwhelming aromas of frankincense and mint, announced that this was, indeed, the first royal Soulai had encountered face-to-face.

"What does it say here?" The boy was still tapping the tag.

Soulai flushed. Although he had been told the tag's

meaning, he couldn't specifically decipher the wedge-shaped characters. And that was the point, wasn't it? This boy was reminding him that he was only a slave, as stupid as an animal, of no more importance than dust itself. Anger stirred within him.

He glared at the face that might nearly have been his own had he been born in the palace. The same shock of black hair arched over a similarly narrow brow. The same raisin-brown eyes sat a little too close alongside a slim nose. But this boy's locks were crimped into neat curls, and a light powder coated his skin. Fine hairs seemed to sprout over the thin upper lip, though it could have been the shadows. Soulai knew his own face had yet to show signs of manhood.

"What does it say here?" the boy insisted petulantly.

"I am told it says my name," he responded in a resentful tone, "and that of another, Habasle. Is that you?"

The prince grinned at the sound of his name. "A welcome surprise: You're smarter than you look. So as not to disillusion me, Soulai, don't open your mouth again. Unless I order it. Now, set rugs on two horses, one of them being this parti-color, and meet me outside. The lion is waiting." With a haughty jerk of his chin, and the confident air that he'd be obeyed, the prince turned and strode down the stable aisle. The two archers exchanged knowing looks and followed obediently, the mastiffs galloping past them.

Choking on humiliation, Soulai darted toward the tack room. The keeper was barely awake, hunched against the wall, cradling a clay cup of steaming brew. He pretended not to hear Soulai's pleadings until Habasle's name was mentioned, and then the cup was set down so abruptly that half the liquid splashed out onto the floor. Soulai loaded his arms with bridles and rugs and their attendant cruppers and breast-collars. On his staggering journey back down the aisle he still managed to scoop up some barley hay for Ti and the stocky bay gelding tethered next to him. The others whinnied jealously, but they would have to wait. Soulai didn't know which he feared more: the wrath of Mousidnou, or that of his surprisingly young owner, Habasle.

Ti was nosing aside the hay to get the last of his grain; a wary eye rolled askance as Soulai slipped in beside him. "Easy, there," Soulai said as he placed the black-fringed rug behind Ti's withers. He smoothed away the wrinkles, then cautiously bent under Ti's belly to fasten the girth. As he fitted the breast-collar, Soulai realized his fingers were shaking. Anger or fear? he asked himself. Inside, he knew the answer.

He well remembered the panicked bleating of his

father's two goats as they'd crumpled in the jaws of the lion. Again he saw the flash of fangs, the bloody lips. And the most frightening part? He'd never even heard the lion coming.

He slipped the bridle over Ti's head, though Ti insisted on continuing to eat, and moved on to the bay gelding. Soulai wondered if he'd be able to stay seated on the horse. He'd sat on a donkey's back more than a few times, but never a horse and never at a gallop. Quickly he offered up a prayer that the bay be steady. And speedy.

"Here!"

Soulai jumped and the girth fell away.

"What in the name of Nergal are you doing?" It was Mousidnou this time, stomping along with his lantern. He peered into the mostly empty trough and squinted his small eyes at Soulai. "These horses haven't even been fed."

Soulai caught the girth and pulled it tight around the bay's belly, his back hunched, prepared for the blow. "Habasle ordered these two made ready," he said. He quickly adjusted the breast-collar and crupper. "Habasle said the lion is waiting."

"Oh." Mousidnou seemed to accept this event as nothing out of the ordinary. "Didn't see the runty little master of the hunt come through. His dogs with him?"

Soulai managed a nod as he kneed the gelding in the belly one more time and pulled the girth tighter. He was not going to slip from this horse's back.

The stable master shook his head. "Can't tell if it's bravery or folly drives that boy." He looked at Soulai, the sharpness suddenly colored by concern. "Listen to me. You watch yourself today."

Soulai had untied the bay and was fitting the bit between his teeth. He paused and looked up.

"I'll deny every word if you survive to repeat it," Mousidnou continued, "but I'm telling you now that Habasle chews through young stable hands the way his dogs chew through hares. After the last incident I thought he'd given up the horses, but . . ." He shrugged, then cast an appreciative eye over Ti. "Shame if he injures this one, though. Sure, he shows promise, but it's too soon for lions."

The throaty barking of the mastiffs traveled down the stable aisle and Mousidnou shot an urgent look at Soulai. "I'll see that your horses are fed. You be off," he said. "Here's a leg up." Setting down his lantern, he boosted Soulai onto the gelding's back. Then Mousidnou backed Ti into the aisle. He handed the reins to Soulai and gruffly patted the boy's leg. "Keep your wits about you now," he warned.

A HUNT 5

Ignorant of the morning's danger, Ti pranced in the narrow aisle. He playfully dove at the bay's neck, once, twice, and was threatening again when Soulai snapped the reins, signaling the stallion to behave. Soulai fully intended to keep his wits about him and he'd do his best to make certain Ti did as well. Knuckles tight around the gelding's reins, legs squeezing his barrel, Soulai pulled Ti's head close to his thigh, and they began moving toward the pink square of light at the end of the stable.

In the courtyard, Soulai found Habasle ringed by a dozen tall, bearded archers. The mastiffs were now leashed, though the slaves restraining them had to use both hands and the weight of their bodies to hold them back. Ti whinnied loudly and the gelding echoed him.

Something pale and billowy dangled from Habasle's fist as he strode across the tiles. He took Ti's reins from

Soulai, then lowered the stallion's head and fastened a decoration to the top of the bridle. When Ti lifted his head, a white plume stood erect, and silky black fringe cascaded over his brow, framing his gold and blue eyes. He looked every shekel a regal horse of the hunt and Soulai shivered with a mixture of pride and dread. Next, Habasle replaced the reins with intricately braided ones specially weighted with pom-poms to ensure that they dropped evenly on either side of Ti's neck. Then he stepped back, nodded approvingly, and, in one graceful move, leaped onto the stallion. Soulai frowned at the bronze spurs he spotted tied to the young nobleman's sandals. Ti hardly required motivation. Lifting his arm in the air, Habasle led the way out of the courtyard. The archers, the mastiffs, and Soulai followed obediently.

Soulai knew he should relax astride his mount; he just couldn't make his body do it. His fingers gripped both reins as well as a good hank of mane. And his knees kept searching for a niche to lock into. But when something in the half-light caused the bay to snort and dance sideways, Soulai not only managed to stay on, but also to rein the animal back in line. For a moment the pleasure of sitting atop such a powerful creature quelled his own trembling.

The early morning entourage left the palace through a massive gate, traveling down the curving ramp and along the walled passageway, which was eerily empty in the predawn. The zoo's animals remained silent, as if they sensed the hunters. As they skirted the market-place, where vendors were just arriving, Soulai caught the whiff of meat grilling. The aroma, normally entic-ing, stirred his unsettled stomach to nausea.

One of Nineveh's fifteen gates loomed ahead and the line halted while Habasle spoke to two guards. Soulai heard his voice rise in a sharp, arrogant tone, then saw the men abruptly step back and let Habasle pass. One by one they filed through the arched opening in the thick inner wall, then passed through the well-guarded outer one. Ishtar, the goddess of Nineveh, protected her city well, Soulai thought as he rode through the tunnel of bricks.

As soon as they had crossed the moat, Habasle turned south. A grassy plain stretched before them, rolling gen-tly toward the ribbon of trees lining the Tigris River to the west and the manicured banks of the Khosr directly ahead. A hazy yellow sun had blossomed behind the city's jagged silhouette; a breath of warm air touched Soulai's neck.

So far, no one except Habasle had spoken. The archers walked behind him in pairs, while the houndsmen fol-lowed, struggling with every step to control the two mastiffs. Soulai brought up the rear. He noted that

Habasle frequently glanced over his shoulder, but when he himself did so, he saw nothing. There was no time to ponder the matter for, just as they were climbing a small rise, a lion's throaty roar split the morning like thunder.

Both horses snorted and Soulai jumped. Habasle calmly motioned for Soulai to move forward and for the archers to fan out on either side of him.

Atop the rise, Soulai looked down upon a wooden crate set amid the emptiness of the flatland. A piteously small slave stood uncertainly beside it; another crouched on top of it. Soulai recognized the crate as the one he had seen dragged in and out of the zoo, and he guessed its occupant. Another roar sounded and the wooden box rattled. The man on top jumped off, saw Habasle, and climbed back on, where he huddled like a frightened rabbit.

Motioning for Soulai to stay put, Habasle led the archers down the slope. The barking mastiffs followed, dragging the handlers in their wake. After some two hundred paces, the procession stopped; the men pulled arrows from their quivers and knelt in the yellowed grasses.

Suddenly Habasle turned and cantered back. Soulai envied how well Ti behaved for him.

"You ride at my side," his owner called when he got

close, "but stay out of my aim. It'll go like this: I'll drop my arm and the lion will be released. In a count of three, the dogs will be released. Once they engage the lion, I'll ride forward, you at my side—but out of my way—understand?" Soulai forced a nod. "I'll dispatch the lion with my spear, straight down his gullet. I don't know this horse—"

"Ti," Soulai offered.

Habasle glared and Soulai remembered the warning about not speaking. He swallowed hard. "The horse is young, I know," his owner went on, "but I'm told he's bred for this." Ti's ears remained pricked toward the crate and Soulai saw one shiver after another ripple his body. Anticipation or fear? Ti's jaws ground his bit so furiously that foam speckled his gold and white chest. Habasle laid a hand on the stallion's withers. "If he tries to bolt when we close in, you're to grab onto the reins and hold him steady while I aim. If the lion gets him, you're to jump down and I'll take your horse. Understand?"

Somehow Soulai forced another nod. A shiver not unlike Ti's shook his own body.

"Let's begin then," Habasle said as he urged Ti down the slope toward the dogs and archers. Soulai tightened his reins and followed. The sweat beneath his thighs was making his seat frighteningly slippery. He shifted position, tried to dig his knees into the hollow behind the bay's elbows, and hoped he'd be able to hang on.

Beyond the crate, distant trees seemed to beckon. Come and hide, they seemed to motion, and for a fleeting moment Soulai thought about clapping his heels to his mount's sides and galloping far away from the lion, maybe even away from Nineveh! But overwhelming fear froze him from action and he proceeded stiffly behind his owner.

Both slaves had now climbed atop the crate and they crouched, clutching the front panel, their faces turned obediently toward Habasle, waiting. The lion roared again, but this time no one, not even those who could feel the heat of his breath, moved. Slowly Habasle lifted his arm and held it there—halting long enough for Soulai to hear the clear cry of a coot upon the river. Then he dropped it.

Groaning in unison, the slaves raised the heavy panel and cowered behind it. The magnificent, black-maned lion spun within the crate—but could not find its captors. Ears flattened, the big cat crept tentatively into the open. The door thudded back into place just as the mastiffs were unleashed, and in an instant the three tangled in a barking, snarling knot that shattered the morning calm.

"Now!" Habasle shouted. He loosed Ti's reins, leveled his spear, and charged. Soulai reluctantly urged his own mount forward. I'm going to die, he thought as they neared the vicious animals. Habasle began circling the fray, tightening the diameter with each lap.

With a loud yelp, one of the mastiffs scooted free, dragging his leg. Habasle leaned in and jabbed at the lion's face. But the agile feline lithely evaded the spear. Screaming with fury, it coiled and sprang at its attacker. Habasle barely managed to pull his leg out from under the deadly claws, which sank instead into Ti's shoulder, ripping loose a sheet of hide. The stallion screamed and leaped backward, only to stumble over the remaining mastiff.

Frantically, Soulai rushed the bay close to the falling pair, aware that the archers were also running forward. But when the injured mastiff returned to the fight, distracting the lion, Ti managed to get his feet beneath him. Habasle recovered his seat and, ignoring the bloody skin flapping from the stallion's shoulder, began circling the animals once more. The archers halted and knelt.

Ti's eyes rolled white with fear. He hopped sideways and strained against the bit to escape. But Habasle gouged him with his spurs, forcing him back to the battle. A wave of cold nausea swept over Soulai: He was going to watch Ti be killed!

The lion and the mastiffs bled so much now from gushing wounds that the fight's tempo slowed. The dogs circled, the cat snarled and swatted. Habasle saw another opening and spurred Ti in close. When he pricked the lion's back, it spun, roaring, and Habasle thrust the weapon straight at its mouth. But the spearhead became tangled in the thick mane, and, with one agile tug, the lion pulled the shaft from Habasle's hand.

Soulai couldn't tear his eyes away from the lion. Horror-stricken, he watched the enormous white fangs clamp down on the spear, saw the huge paw reach up and snap it into pieces with one swat. With his heart in his mouth, Soulai saw the newly enraged creature charge the dogs, give each a lightning-quick swipe, then turn and crouch to pounce again upon his human assailant.

Having no weapon, Habasle panicked. Before Soulai realized it, the prince had jumped onto the gelding's back. "Get off!" he screamed in Soulai's ear. The force of the lion's lunge knocked Ti backward and, as if in a nightmare, Soulai saw that the cat had wrapped its claws around the stallion's neck and shoulders and was trying to bring him down.

Ti's screams of terror pierced Soulai's heart. The stallion was falling, and without thinking, Soulai leaned over and straddled him. Thick saliva splashed onto

Soulai's legs a moment before claws ripped down his thigh. The pain was even hotter than that of the branding iron. But Soulai shunted it aside to focus on jerking Ti's head around and kicking him with the leg he could still feel. "Try!" he screamed into Ti's ear, tearing at the bit and pummeling the ribs with one heel. "Try!"

But the stallion kept stumbling and Soulai knew they were going down together. Somewhere amid the confusion he heard the lion roar with fresh pain and knew it was releasing its hold. Ti staggered a few more steps, free now of the giant cat's weight, then began to right himself. Soulai didn't pause. He kept tugging on the bit and kicking the blood-slickened sides to urge the stallion away from the battle. Finally, after what seemed a lifetime, he felt Ti begin to move forward. He aimed the horse's head for the trees and let him bolt.

Only when they were far into the underbrush did Soulai pull Ti to a stop. The stallion was so panicked that he wouldn't stand still. He spun crazily in circles, his eyes rolling, searching for the lion, until Soulai fell off, gasping when his own injured leg hit the ground. The broken feather, spattered bright red, drooped across Ti's ears. Soulai tore it away in disgust.

Another horse's screams rent the air. Filled with dread, Soulai managed to lead Ti back through the underbrush toward the field. He reached it just in time to see the bay gelding fall under the lion's weight. Habasle was scrambling free and sprinting away. The archers advanced, firing arrows as they ran. Two sank into the lion's hide, another missed and embedded itself in the gelding. The dogs' handlers were moving in, too, whistling for the mastiffs to retreat. Soon it was only the archers and the lion and a storm of arrows. The lion collapsed upon the downed horse, who lay quivering. One of the archers ran up and, drawing a knife from his sheath, jabbed it between the horse's jawbones. The bay fell quiet.

Habasle stomped back toward the two bodies, angrily waving away the archers. He held an unbroken spear in his hand. One by one he began tugging the arrows from the lion's carcass and tossing them aside. Then he plunged his spear deep into the chest of the dead lion. He turned, triumphant. "I am Habasle!" he shouted.

THE LEOPARD'S
BROKEN LEG

A sudden need to cough brought Soulai to consciousness. The ensuing hacking made him acutely aware of the dusty closeness of his room, and of a thick, over-sweet taste coating his tongue. What had happened? He blinked, tried to wrap his mind around something that made sense, but a soothing drowsiness pulled him back into slumber.

Again he awoke. This time he struggled to sit up. Thunder in his head—and a knifing pain in his leg—forced him down. He groaned. The rope of light outlining the room's crooked door glowed with the haze of early morning. Or late afternoon. Which was it?

A bandage cuffed his thigh and Soulai's fingers blindly probed the coarse cloth. He began to remember the slave woman who had treated him. She had tended him with few words, for she spoke a language he didn't understand. The woman had splashed his raw wounds with water, then wrapped them in cotton bandages. It was she who had held a ladle of dark syrup to his lips, a liquid that barely disguised its bitter root. After that he remembered nothing.

As Soulai shook off the drugged stupor, bloody images began to emerge from his mind. He remembered Habasle and the hunt—if you could call it that. He remembered the lion. And Ti. Soulai bolted upright. He had to get to the stable.

Clenching his teeth so hard that the ache in his jaws battled the throbbing in his head, Soulai climbed to his feet and managed to hobble to the door before crying out. He didn't dare sit down, for he knew he wouldn't get up. Nausea prickled his insides, yet he leaned into the door and pushed it open. He stumbled through it and over to a low wall. One hand gripped the warm bricks, the other hovered protectively over his bandaged thigh. Vaguely aware that people stared, he continued weaving his way toward the stable.

By the time he reached it, Soulai was drenched in sweat. One glance told him it was the afternoon feeding. As he turned down the aisle stabling his ten horses, he discovered Mousidnou. The man's usual scowl had been replaced with a somber expression that bordered on sadness. He was holding a knife in one hand and a ragged piece of golden hide in the other. Soulai panicked. His eyes darted over the rumps, counting, searching. A blessed relief washed over him as he found the silvery hindquarters. Ti was alive.

The sweat cooled, chilling him, as he hobbled toward the stable master.

"All day and that damned asu still hasn't shown himself," Mousidnou muttered to no one in particular. He lifted the limp skin and made a face. "Seems like the thing to do—it's no use now." Looking up and down the aisle, past the labors of his stable boys, Mousidnou suddenly seemed to realize Soulai's presence. With a brusque nod toward the bandaged leg, he asked, "How is it?"

But Soulai was intent on reaching Ti. Ignoring his own pain, he slipped in beside the stallion, tugged on the tether, and lowered his face to the drooping head. No response, not even a nip. He cradled the white jowl in his hand, shuddered at its lifeless cold. The gold eye and the blue eye, each half-lidded, stared dully. The wide nostrils fluttered with rapid, shallow breaths.

"Habasle's been here," Mousidnou said louder.

"He's a cur," Soulai spat.

The stable master's eyebrows shot up. "He's your owner, boy. Watch he doesn't bite." He wiped the bloody blade of the knife on his tunic and resheathed it.

"Habasle was near pissed as you when I told him the asu hadn't come—stomped off to find the man himself. Said he'd bring an ashipu as well, though I don't know that he'll see to an animal."

Soulai ducked beneath Ti's neck. He cringed at the raw flesh bubbling a yellow ooze. Flies waded through the stuff and he waved them away, but they returned in force to settle into the hairless folds and crevices. Seeing the strands of mane stuck to the pink flesh, he gently tried to pull them out. Ti grunted weakly, then let out a long breath and dropped his head lower.

Soulai gasped. "Can't you do something?" he begged Mousidnou.

"Huh," the stable master snorted. "I've been to the battle more than a few times. Killed my share of men and cleaned up my share of horses." He glanced at the flap of skin still dangling from his fist. "But when the demons come for what's theirs . . ." He shook his head. "I don't meddle with Nergal's underworld."

Voices sounded from down the aisle and the two looked up to see Habasle and a smallish, bald man in an ankle-length tunic and robe marching toward them. A lion's limp paws draped Habasle's neck. The man clutched a leather pouch to his chest like a shield.

"It is this horse," Habasle pronounced as they reached Ti. His slap on Ti's rump produced no more response than the thudding sound of hand against meat. "He is of value to me and you must make him live."

The asu glanced at Soulai, who was still stroking Ti's head. A tenderness was visible in the man's eyes, which gave Soulai a glimmer of hope.

"Get out!"

The abrupt command came from Habasle, and Soulai didn't have to question for whom it was meant. Head dutifully lowered, he slid along the stallion's flanks and, careful not to brush against him, past the person responsible for Ti's misery. His nose wrinkled at the pungent scent of freshly bathed skin and perfumed hair. How I hate him! he thought as his fists tightened. Trembling with pain and anger, Soulai waited beside Mousidnou.

The asu pursed his lips and gently laid his hands on Ti. With slow, thoughtful movements he examined the crusted, reddish-brown scratches. When he came to the gaping wound on Ti's neck and shoulder, he clucked his tongue and reached into his pouch.

Carrying a handful of dried sprigs out to the aisle, the asu knelt, struck his flint, and ignited them. He muttered something into the fire, then dug through his pouch again. This time he pulled out a wood bowl into which he poured a whitish powder. Adding a handful of animal fat, he worked the mixture several minutes with his fingers, then stood and carried the bowl toward Ti. As the salve was pressed into his neck wound, Ti came to life, bucking and snorting.

Instinctively Soulai lunged, but Mousidnou's iron grip on his arm stopped him.

Ti's eyes rolled to white. With his head strongly tethered, though, and escape impossible, he fell to heaving his weight from side to side.

The asu kept a calm, yet wary eye on the shifting stallion, stepping away as needed, but always returning to daub more of his sticky concoction into the freshly oozing wound. When the bowl was near empty, he returned to his pouch to pull forth coiled cotton bandages. He began wrapping what he could of the shoulder, as well as the horse's neck, so tightly that Soulai himself had trouble swallowing.

The tail of the last bandage was still dangling when another man, unusually tall, came striding down the aisle. Like Habasle, he wore a robe of noble length, but his was blood red. A voluminous leather pouch was slung across his shoulder, the straps clamping down on a huge gold medallion. The asu's eyes widened and he looked as if he wanted to flee.

"This is the beast?"

"Yes," Habasle answered regally. "You are ordered to attend him."

The man cocked his head, examining Habasle with barely disguised disdain. Soulai noticed that his eyes were completely black, as if both pupils had exploded and frozen. "Ah, then," he said, "we must—no, no, no! Those bandages are all wrong." In one step and with a great flourish of robes he began tearing away the asu's careful work. "Such haphazardry might suffice in Elam, but we follow the scholars' methods in this land."

The smallish man shuffled aside. "You are the ashipu," he murmured. "I will watch and learn." The others appeared to bow to this forceful man as well, but Soulai had a strong sense that Ti would have fared better with the asu. And when the red-robed man, in one yank, tore the sticky mane from the exposed wound, ripping a squeal from the stallion, it took both of Mousidnou's hands to hold Soulai to his place.

The ashipu bent close to the moist flesh and sniffed. "Alum?"

"In sheep's lard," the asu replied.

The tall man nodded. "Adequate." Picking up the bandages, he deftly rolled them around his thin hand and began wrapping Ti's neck again. Soulai couldn't tell the difference from the way the asu had wrapped them in the first place.

"You are the stable master, are you not?" The ashipu was speaking with no less disdain to Mousidnou now, who nodded quickly. "Trim the frog of the right front hoof, then." He stepped aside.

Grunting, Mousidnou bent over his ample belly to lift Ti's hoof and slice a section from the leathery center, which he handed to the ashipu. The man dropped it into the ashes. Another spark, a small flame, and the moon-shaped piece started to shrivel. Before it was consumed, however, the ashipu plucked it out and ground it up in his own small bowl. Then, poking the powder into a reed, the tall man walked to Ti's head, grasped an ear, and blew the dust into it.

He held the long fingers of his right hand splayed across the frightened horse's forehead, holding him magically captive. The man's eyelids fluttered, then closed. "O Ishtar, goddess of Nineveh," the ashipu prayed, "let the might of this steed's hooves pound out the evil that threatens to drive him from the light of this world. O Shamash, exalted in this land, let not the claw of a lion fell this royal creature, but let your mighty hand spare his life that he may see out his number of days and gallop toward the destiny that you alone have determined."

The ashipu opened his eyes. His gaze fell upon Habasle and his lips curled as he reached out to lift one of the lion's paws. "Killed by your own hand?"

"I thrust my spear into him."

The man let the paw drop. "Your mother will be proud."

"I'd rather my father know the pride."

The ashipu folded his arms, looked down his hooked nose, and blinked. "But we'll never know if your father knows, will we, since we don't know in which alley he sleeps?"

Habasle grasped the hilt of his knife. "My father is King Ashurbanipal."

"So says your mother," the ashipu responded with a sneer. Out of thin air a knife appeared in his own hand and he held it high between them. He twisted the blade in the fiery light of the newly lit lanterns. "A claw," he said, and slashed a toe from the lion's foot. Soulai heard Mousidnou exhale as the ashipu turned toward Ti and knotted the claw in his mane. And he noted Habasle's chest rising and falling beneath the limp paws, though his face displayed a rigid calm.

The asu was studying the ashipu's bandaging when he called to the others. "Have you seen this?" he asked. "This mark on his other shoulder? Doesn't it look like the wings of a hawk? I believe he's been blessed by Ninurta himself."

Before anyone could move closer, though, Ti let out a long groan and sank to the bedding. Soulai shot a panicked look at Mousidnou. "The evil spirits," the stable master whispered in explanation. "Doing battle with the gods." He watched the horse and he shook his head. "Not many a man, let alone an animal, lives through this."

Ti's sudden collapse brought back the ashipu's scowl. He folded his bony frame into a crouching position over the small fire, pulled fragrant leaves from his dark pouch, and tossed them into the flames. Now his invocation seemed more in earnest.

"O Ninurta," he spoke, "god of the hunt, god of war, grant that the wounds of this noble horse, one of your hallowed creatures and faithful servants, may heal. Grant that this animal may once again shine as a servant to his god, the one that has marked him in his own image, and that he may gallop over the land trumpeting the glorious name of Ninurta."

The flames slowly died out. The horse didn't get up. "That is all I can do," the ashipu announced. He stood and walked away. After an awkward silence, the asu followed.

Soulai glared at his owner's back. Habasle turned and coolly looked Soulai up and down.

"Your leg has been tended, I see, so you're well enough to keep an eye on this horse. Stay with him." He looked at Mousidnou. "Summon me if he gets worse." Without so much as a final glance at Ti, Habasle followed the others out. Soulai noticed him hesitate at the doorway, though, saw him look each way before proceeding across the courtyard.

"I hate him," Soulai muttered between clenched teeth. "I hate him! He'll never touch Ti again if I have a say in it."

Mousidnou coughed up a big wad of spittle and projected it across the aisle. "As if you could have a say in it, you clod. You're forgetting your place—and that's more dangerous than any lion." He glanced at Soulai's bandaged thigh. "Do you know the story 'After the Hunt'?"

Soulai shook his head.

"Plague it!" The stable master cleared his throat again, looked both ways down the aisle, and repeated his curse. "Well, boy, as there's a long night before the both of us, or the three of us," he said, nodding toward the silent stallion, "do you good to hear it. Maybe if you clean that wax out of your ears you'll learn something." He took a deep breath and began.

"It so happens that one day, just before sunup, a lion, a leopard, and a jackal decide to join in a little hunting. And before the day is even warm they get themselves a fine catch: a boar, an antelope, and a duck. Now the leopard and the jackal, they're so hungry that they're licking their lips and circling their prizes and planning where they'll begin; but the lion, he jumps up with a loud growl and stares them both down. 'There's a lot of meat here,' he says. 'Leopard, you divide it as you see fit.'

"Now the leopard isn't expecting this. In fact, he's already planning how to get the dead antelope up into a tree where he can take his time eating it. So without much thought he says, 'Lion, you eat the boar, I'll take the antelope, and the jackal can have the duck.'

"Well, the lion swats him so hard that the leopard finds himself limping away with a broken leg. 'Jackal,' the lion roars, 'you divide the meat!'

"Now the jackal, being the cunning survivor that he is, has been watching carefully. Quick as lightning, he drags both the boar and the antelope over to the lion and bows as he backs away. 'I believe that is the lion's share,' he says. 'With your permission, the leopard and I will share the duck.'

"The lion rumbles with pleasure. 'How, my friend, did you learn to share so well?'

"'I took a lesson from the leopard's broken leg!' he says."

Mousidnou paused. He looked pleased with himself. "I'm warning you," he said, "no matter what you or I think of Habasle, he is the lion, son of King Ashurbanipal and—"

"The ashipu doesn't seem to think—"

The knuckled side of the stable master's hand cracked across Soulai's face. "Listen, you snot-nosed little turd. I don't know why I'm blowing words into your thick skull, except that your ass is hitched to Habasle's, so you'd better understand his situation." He lifted his hand again, hesitated, and lowered it. "It's like this. Soon after Habasle's mother came to the palace, still a girl, she had a child, Habasle. She claimed to have lain with the king, but at about that time it was also discovered that a slave boy had been sneaking into the harem. My wife tells me that in the fourteen years since Habasle's birth, his mother has lain with the king many times but has not conceived. So palace tongues wag that this is proof that Habasle isn't royal, that he's the son of the slave who escaped long ago.

"And, as this seems to be my evening for counseling asses," the stable master continued, "I'll tell you this. The palace runs thick with rumors—some true, most false—all stirred up to sweeten one's position." His fist found the hilt of his knife as his eyes narrowed. "It was never like this on the battlefield. There, wagging tongues were silenced. But here, the fact of the matter is that King Ashurbanipal has many sons, and only one will be king after him. A mother's love for her own son can, shall we say, breed lies. Now," Mousidnou said, smoothing his tunic over his protruding belly, "you can

66

burn some of that misplaced anger of yours feeding and watering your horses. And no whimpering like some whipped puppy." He jerked his head toward Ti. "He's got it a lot tougher than you."

"I'm not complaining," Soulai called out in the direction of Mousidnou's retreating back. "And I'm not leaving. I'm sleeping here."

The lumbering man shrugged. "I'll send my wife with something later," he answered.

The moment Mousidnou was out of sight, half a dozen stable boys left their tasks to flock around Soulai. Their questions sounded like the chatter of crows. On another day Soulai might have relished telling of the morning's hunt, perhaps even exaggerating his bravery. But now, all Soulai could do was look past the boys to Ti, who lay miserable and unmoving, his massive haunches slack, his silken tail drooping. Only the tether's length kept Ti's head from resting full cheek in the manure. As it was, powdery dung cupped his muzzle. So Soulai said nothing. And one by one the stable boys fell silent and crept back to their duties.

By the time Soulai had led the last horse from the water trough, the three brilliant stars of the summer triangle shone overhead, the great bird with the outstretched wings soaring through their midst. He reentered the stable, knotted the final tether, and, trembling with fatigue and a tremendous throbbing, lowered himself onto the aisle floor. A stab of pain made him dig his fingers into the crevice between the bricks and the wall. To his surprise, he found the familiar grittiness of clay. Scraping up a small amount with his index finger, he wadded it into a ball. Slowly he began coaxing a small horse from the lump, all the while staring at Ti's silvery silhouette.

"How is it?" came an unfamiliar voice.

Soulai started, for he hadn't heard anyone approach. He looked up to find a pear-shaped woman with graying hair gathered at the nape of her neck standing beside him. She was holding a basket covered by a cloth.

"Your leg, how is it?" she repeated. "Can you walk?"

Soulai nodded, then looked back at Ti. The woman followed his gaze.

"He looks bad," she said gently.

"He is bad," Soulai whispered. "I think he's leaving the light."

She folded her hands and waited in silence.

Near to tears, Soulai found himself pouring out his thoughts. "He said Ti had value to him, but where is he now? He's just left him here to die. He doesn't see . . ." His voice cracked. "He only sees what he wants to see," he finished.

Refusing to cry, Soulai blinked hard and stared

straight ahead. He wasn't aware how much time had passed before it came to him that this woman must be Mousidnou's wife and that she had already tiptoed away, leaving the basket of figs and flatbread at his side. The clay figurine remained unfinished in his lap. The hush of night fell over the palace and still he didn't move. Only when the jackals gathered around Nineveh's gates to yelp their eerie songs did a shiver run the length of his body.

"Please," he whispered to the demons haunting the black air, "please don't take him."

CRY AND 7 ANSWER

Each night, the constellation of the great bird soared a little farther across the night sky. Each day, from the month of Ab to the month of Elul, burned a little hotter. Nineveh's palace shimmered in the stifling heat. Yellowed leaves fell from the potted trees and lay motionless until a sudden hot wind swept them, tinkling, across the tiled courtyards. Dry as the desert, the wind and the heat sucked life from every living thing, and the normal palace bustle died to sluggish steps.

The horses and soldiers continued to train, however. Word had come that the Medes were mounting a challenge to Assyria's borders. As Soulai looked over the armory's training grounds one afternoon, he saw and heard a heightened urgency that defied the heat. His eyes scanned pairs of lathered horses pulling heavy, two-wheeled chariots, the drivers' shouts of encouragement punctuating the slap of reins. Raucous barking and growling caught his attention as the royal keeper of the hounds tossed chunks of meat over the heads of his mastiffs. But Soulai was searching for something else—someone else, actually—and he knew he was within sight.

"We'll take them over there," Mousidnou interrupted. Soulai followed the stable master toward the dappled shade of a large acacia bush. The horses they were leading lowered their heads to nibble the scant grasses.

Shielding his eyes from the dust and sun, Soulai continued to survey the center of the grounds where hundreds of soldiers, horses, and slaves milled about between scattered piles of weapons and shields. Some of the men practiced hand-to-hand combat under the watchful eyes of instructors. Others took turns on the horses, spearing targets with their lances, then charging each other with blunt poles. In one of these clusters, the young men were outfitted in the pale blue and white of royalty. That was where Soulai picked out the boy who owned him.

"Look at him," he muttered as he watched Habasle aim his pole at a mounted opponent and spur his horse into a charge. "He's practically gagging that horse."

Mousidnou observed, but didn't say anything. The combatants missed each other on the first pass, spun, and charged again. In the next clash Habasle's opponent grabbed the wobbling end of Habasle's pole and flipped it skyward, knocking Habasle off his horse. Habasle jumped up, yelling, and a commander galloped over to intervene.

Mousidnou grunted. "Loudest of the litter he is, always yapping he didn't get a fair chance at the teat."

"Fair chance?" Soulai complained. "He doesn't know what fair is. He *owns* people and horses and dogs, and . . . and he doesn't care if they live, or die a slow death, as long as he gets his way." He watched Habasle vault onto his mount, jerk the reins so hard that the horse's mouth gaped, then cockily trot back toward a servant who handed him a new pole. Soulai turned away, his face flushed with anger.

He focused his attention instead on the horse he led— Ti. Although gray scabs curled from the cuts on his flanks, the wound at the base of his neck continued to fester and the stallion moved stiffly. For the first weeks of the month of Ab, weeks without sleep, Soulai had cared for Ti. At least four times a day he had lugged fresh water from the courtyard trough and, between chores, had sneaked away to pull tender grasses from the canals. He'd once even risked losing a hand by stealing an apple from a silver tray. Ti had barely fluttered his nostrils at the treat.

While the gods of life and death had fought over his

spirit, the horse's body had sweated and shivered in endless rounds. He had finally fallen so weak that even when the battle was over and won, he could hardly nibble the handfuls of grain Soulai had cupped beneath his muzzle. His hide had shrunk to reveal ribs and hips and each bumpy bone of his spine. Soulai had starved with him. How could he eat when Ti was dying?

Kneeling beside him each night, Soulai stroked the horse's flanks, mumbling prayers and pouring out his love. He touched the crest of Ti's drooping neck, let his fingers skim down the broad forehead and across the veins of his cheek. There was no punishing nip. As he memorized each facet of the stallion's face, Soulai felt the creative fire returning to his hands. He recalled that he had once been able to breathe life into shapeless clay, and the rhythm of his strokes quickened. With keen concentration, then, he began kneading and rubbing and polishing Ti's body, willing the spark of life to take hold.

Gradually the animal's appetite improved, and after some time he was able to stand for the greater part of the day. Soulai heaved a sigh of relief, yet one that was not completely without worry. For while he had been able to rub a shine back into Ti's coat, the horse's spirit remained lackluster. He did prick his ears now when Soulai approached, and he even sounded an occasional nicker of gratitude, but otherwise he showed no interest in the world around him. It was Mousidnou who had suggested that before the evening's chores a walk outside the stable might do the stallion good.

A rising cheer from the grounds caused the horse that Mousidnou led to lift his head, but Ti only cocked an ear. The head charioteer had loosed his blue-black stallions along the armory's curving inside track and the driver nearest him was urging his pair into the contest. The two men exchanged grins as they slapped their reins and their teams stretched into a pounding gallop. Shouts erupted from the soldiers as the horses took a dangerously wide sweep around the end of the grounds, scattering dogs and men. They raced wheel to wheel the length of the field, careened around the far turn, and came charging up on the rows of chariots in training maneuvers. Several of the horses in harness reared and bucked in attempts to join the gallop.

The teams slowed. The race was over and the two men reined their horses into line with the front row of chariots. Just as both teams came to a blowing, prancing walk, however, the head charioteer whistled to his horses and they sprang again into full gallop, leaving a thick cloud of dust over their challenger.

The dark stallions came surging around the turn again, and this time pulled to a halt right in front of

Soulai and Mousidnou. Ti shied away. As Soulai soothed him with a calming hand, he admired the magnificent, sweat-slickened animals harnessed to the chariot. Their manes, shiny as the feathers of a glossy ibis, fell from bulging crests. The whites of their eyes flashed as they tossed their heads and champed their bits. Every muscle in their bodies was chiseled like a warrior's.

Mousidnou congratulated the charioteer, who grinned and nodded respectfully in return. But the smile vanished when he saw Ti.

"Isn't this the young stallion marked by Ninurta?" He jumped out of his chariot, tossing a look of alarm at Soulai as he stomped past. "I thought I told you to look after him!" Ti responded to the agitation by snorting and pulling away, and the man wisely slowed his approach. He circled the nervous animal, shaking his head as he took in the injuries. "What in the name of the wind demon happened?"

Soulai looked to Mousidnou in a silent plea for help, but the stable master remained stone-faced.

"Well?" the charioteer demanded. "How did you let this happen, boy?"

"It was a lion, but I didn't—" Soulai began.

"A lion? You took this horse after lions—at his age? By whose order?"

Again Soulai glanced toward Mousidnou, but the man's attention seemed to be focused on other chariot maneuvers.

"Habasle's." Soulai's voice cracked, though a thrill ran through him as he placed the blame.

For all his fury, the charioteer looked more sad than angry. "Do you know what you've done?" He gestured toward Ti. "You've ruined him. One of the king's finest-bred stallions—and you've ruined him before the end of his fourth year."

Each harsh word pierced Soulai like a tiny arrow.

"Just look at his eyes," the man implored. "Remember what I said about the odd-colored ones, how rare they are, how they show courage? Well, look. What do they show now?"

Biting his lip, Soulai looked directly into Ti's eyes. They showed . . .

"Nothing! That's right, nothing. They're weak, dead. *Pfftt!* No fire, no courage. This horse is no better than dog meat now. Cut him up for the mastiffs, Mousidnou, because he's not worth the rope 'round his head."

Soulai winced. It couldn't be true.

"In some fairness," he heard Mousidnou saying, "the boy did save the horse's life by risking his own. And he's tended to him while keeping up his duties, though hardly able to walk himself."

Soulai's tunic hid his own scars, so the charioteer's downward glance found no reason for sympathy. He sneered. "Well, you needn't waste any more time." He shook his head in disgust and stepped into his chariot. Gathering the reins, he leveled a pained look at Soulai. "It seems you and your master have more in common than your looks; you're both careless with a thing of value."

Soulai stood stunned and speechless as the charioteer galloped his horses away. He turned to Mousidnou and barely croaked, "What he said about Ti, is it true?"

The stable master shrugged. "It's his business to know horses," he said. "And it has been more than two weeks, with the animal only a shadow of himself." He paused as he continued scanning the training grounds. "I've watched it happen to warriors as well as warhorses, and my answer would be to give him a chance to live. But whether he has the heart to care about living is the question."

Soulai looked again at Ti, and this time saw with shocking clarity that he looked more like a cheap cart horse than a prize stallion. With tears in his eyes he spun toward the training grounds that Ti would probably never again visit. How he wished for the gods to fling some evil down upon Habasle! He'd destroyed Ti, turned him into dog meat!

He blinked harder and faster and shot a fierce glance across the field. Habasle was galloping again toward an opponent, pole raised. Soulai hurled his hatred at him!

A sharp, sudden cry arose from the commotion. Soulai watched, dumbstruck, as Habasle slumped over his mount's neck, then slid off onto the ground. His opponent's pole seemed to have somehow become tangled in his clothing and Habasle clutched it as he fell. Several of the men paused, waiting for Habasle to get up; then one of the commanders jumped from his horse and ran toward him. He knelt and rolled Habasle onto his back. With a chill, Soulai saw the pole—thrust like a spear into Habasle's side.

The commander shouted orders. Then, with one foot on Habasle, he yanked the pole free. Habasle pulled up his knees, shrieking and writhing in pain. Two men approached, grasped him by the shoulders and ankles, and carried him from the grounds. The commander, examining the pole's tip, continued to shout, this time at the opponent, who spread his arms in a gesture of innocence. Soulai could tell by the commander's anger that innocence had no part in Habasle's misfortune.

Guilt swept over him. A moment before he had wished the worst upon Habasle and now, perhaps, it had happened. Have I killed him? he wondered. Or had someone else not wanted him to live?

"You see," Mousidnou was saying calmly, "the gods have given Habasle many things. But it is like they say in the marketplace: He who possesses much silver may be happy, and he who possesses much barley may be glad, but he who owns nothing at all may, at least, sleep."

DESTINY'S 8 DRAWINGS

"This is the library. Habasle said to wait here."

The child runner who spoke had latched onto Soulai's wrist as Soulai was carrying a basket of dung from the stable and had tugged him on a winding course through the palace grounds. Now, just as abruptly, the boy released it. Without a backward glance, he trotted across the tiles and disappeared into the comings and goings of the other workers.

Soulai waited. He'd spent much of last night and all of today wondering if he'd killed Habasle. Well, he thought, obviously Habasle wasn't dead; so I'm innocent, true? Yet he guiltily fiddled with the clay tag around his neck while watching a beetle crawl atop a wall. He sighed and shifted his weight from one foot to the other. Increasingly anxious, he looked around. But the walkways surrounding the library remained empty.

Still, something, he was certain, was about to happen.

He felt eyes watching him. Again he searched the area—left, right, in front, and behind—and saw no one. But blinking up into the bright sunlight, he caught his breath. Two monstrous stone lamassu glowered above him, their shadowed brows suspending heavy, knotted beards that stretched halfway to their cloven limestone feet. Wings the size of oxcarts shielded their powerful bull's bodies. No matter which way he turned, it seemed, their stern faces followed him.

Soulai crossed his arms and sidled around the corner, out of their sight. Maybe the runner had gotten Habasle's message wrong, he thought; maybe I should return to the stable. The shadows were growing shorter; the morning was almost over and Mousidnou would surely be growling about Soulai's unfinished chores.

He fingered the clay tag again. With a grimace, he admitted he couldn't leave. As much as he hated it, Habasle owned him—owned all his actions—and Habasle had commanded him to come here. He had to wait.

As the empty morning dragged on, Soulai discovered a series of carved stone panels that wrapped the library like a wondrous belt. Each one portrayed an Assyrian victory at war. Such was the talent of the unknown artist that the chiseled figures seemed to act out their stories right before Soulai's eyes.

In one scene, odd-looking men astride camels—two

to a hump—were fleeing the Assyrian army, and archers on foot and horseback pelted the defeated men with arrows. Soulai could almost hear the thunder of hooves, the incessant whine of arrows, and the thud and scream as iron dug into flesh. He peered into the unblinking eye of a man stretched upon the ground, one hand clawing the dirt. An arrow jutted from his shoulder. As if by its own will, Soulai's hand stretched toward the stony shaft. His fingers traced its length to where it pierced the man's skin. He flinched and yanked his hand away. Not realizing he had been holding his breath, he let it out and moved on.

A few panels down, Assyrian soldiers scaled the walls of an enemy city. So frightened were the inhabitants that they leaped from the towers to drown in the river below. The sculptor had carved the naked bodies of men and women mingling with the fishes below the surface of the roiling waters. Soulai shuddered. Would he have had the bravery to jump to his death rather than be taken captive? He remembered his stumbling journey down the mountain beneath Jahdunlim's whip. Jumping to his death had seemed an escape then; but he hadn't, had he? He was a coward in death as well as life.

Running his fingers along the undulating crevices that described the river, he moved to the next panel, another battle scene, the Assyrian army once more victorious. Hundreds of mounted archers trampled the fallen enemy. But these victims, destined to die with the next hoof fall, thrust long spears into the bellies of the horses that rode over them. So while the battle-ground was cluttered with human remains, Soulai noted that scores of horses flailed there as well. His throat tightened as he saw the eyes bulging in pain, the mouths gaping midscream. One horse stumbled on three legs with a broken spear embedded in its chest. Soulai searched the panel for the rider, but could not find him. With a rapid heartbeat he remembered how Habasle had abandoned Ti the instant he was injured. Obviously it was the same in battle. The horse was just another tool, no better than an arrow or a spear, to be flung at the enemy and forgotten.

"What do you wish to know? Only but ask. Only ask. What is it?"

A brisk voice interrupted his thoughts. He turned to find an old man, woolly gray head bound in a silver-embroidered band, clasping his hands to his chest and smiling a toothy grin.

"I am Naboushoumidin," the man said, "chief scribe to King Ashurbanipal and keeper of the royal tablets. I will search for your answer if you will only tell me the question. Any question." He twisted his hands in fid-gety enthusiasm as he smiled. Soulai guessed by the man's flat nose and ample lips that he, too, came from somewhere else, and he was sorry to dampen the enthusiasm in the striking blue eyes.

"I was brought here," he said, "Habasle sent for me."

The scribe's smile disappeared. "Habasle is here again? Not with his dogs!" The fringe of his yellow robe swirled about his ankles as he pivoted and plunged into the shadows of the arching entry. "No, no, no, no, no." Soulai heard him chattering over and over like an angry ground squirrel. "He's not to bring those slobbering beasts into my library."

Rather than continuing to wait, Soulai ducked his head beneath the stony glares of the lamassu and followed. Inside it was one narrow room after another. The flickering oil lamps revealed thousands of clay tablets spilling from every corner. Some were as small as his palm, others as broad as a soldier's shield. Two of the larger rooms contained ornately carved tablets at which young scribes sat, surrounded by hills of still more tablets. Soulai saw that they patiently copied the wedge-shaped marks of the baked tablets onto the moist clay of others. His fingers tingled at the sight, but he hurried after Naboushoumidin. Close on the man's heels, Soulai traveled the maze until they came to a small, unlit room. The rumbling growl of a large dog halted his steps.

The old scribe extended a protective arm across Soulai and they stood motionless until their eyes adjusted to the darkness. Gradually Soulai made out Habasle crouched in the corner, one hand on the collar of a drooling mastiff.

Naboushoumidin cleared his throat. "We've been through this," he began somewhat hesitantly. "You know I cannot—I simply will not—tolerate beasts in my library. These tablets are much too rare. What if one broke? The loss: unimaginable, irreparable, irretrievable! Your father has gone to great lengths to—" He screwed up his face and thrust out a hand. "Give me the dog."

Soulai watched in astonishment as Habasle climbed to his feet and marched the huge animal, hair abristle on its neck and still growling, straight toward the old man. He feared the worst, but Naboushoumidin didn't flinch, just resolutely wrapped his finger around the studded collar, backed out of the room, and, with his arm stiffly extended, said, "I will return him to the keeper of the hounds."

"You will hold him for me at the library's entrance," Habasle ordered.

"As you wish," the scribe murmured without pause.

Habasle snickered as the awkward pair moved away, each equally suspicious of the other. "Naboushoumidin won't dare to breathe for fear Annakum will devour him."

Soulai looked at this boy whom he hated. There was something different about him today. Maybe it was the dim light, but Habasle's face looked sallow beneath his dark curls. And though the air this deep inside the library was cool, sweat beaded his brow. Habasle moved his hand to cradle the lumpy bandage beneath his clothing.

"You were watching yesterday," he said.

Soulai nodded.

"Did you see who did this to me?" He opened his blue and white robe just enough to reveal a blood-spotted tunic.

Soulai wasn't sure how to answer, wasn't sure if he *should* answer.

"Don't tell me you're blind as well as dumb. What did you see?"

Soulai bristled. "I saw you jousting with someone taller," he responded, "maybe older, but I—"

"No," Habasle interrupted. He sank back against the wall, plainly weary. "I know with whom I jousted. I mean, did you see who put the spear tip on the pole? They're supposed to be blunt."

Soulai shook his head.

"You said you were watching," Habasle spoke angrily. "Why weren't you watching *me*? You're my slave; you're supposed to take care of me."

"I . . . I didn't know," Soulai stammered. "I was grazing Ti."

"How is he?"

The question stunned him. Why do you care about Ti? he thought. You're the one who abandoned him to the lion.

Habasle groaned as he lowered himself to the floor. As if he knew Soulai's thoughts, he said, "Haven't you heard? The Medes have taken Harran. That's why I'm here, studying their tactics as they have been recorded. There's going to be a war, you see." He paused for two labored breaths. "The time is coming," he continued, "when Ti and I must prove ourselves. Our fates are woven together. Look, just as he bears the mark of Ninurta—god of the hunt, god of war—upon his shoulder, so do I." With obvious strain, he tugged at the necklines of his robe and tunic, finally managing to pull them down over one shoulder.

Soulai bent to look. A winged image fanned across Habasle's skin, but even in the poor light he could tell that the intricate, reddish lines were only a blurred henna tattoo.

"Do you see it?" Habasle asked. "It's the same as Ti's, isn't it?"

"I see it," Soulai said.

"And it's the same as Ti's."

It was the same arrogance as the lion's in Mousid-nou's story, and Soulai was finding it difficult to play the subservient jackal. He gritted his teeth. How could this pampered ass think he was anything like the noble Ti?

"Tell me what you're thinking; I order it."

Sucking in his breath, Soulai said, "I don't think you can simply draw your own destiny."

To his surprise, Habasle grinned. "Which shows us why you're a slave and I'm the son of a king. Not only am I going to draw my own destiny, I'm going to draw it bigger, and dye it brighter, than old Ashurbanipal himself. I may be only one of his many sons, but with Ti I'm going to prove I'm the best." He coldly appraised Soulai, then snorted. "Look at us, the same years—thirteen . . . fourteen, right?—almost the same bodies, though mine is stronger. We even resemble each other in the face; I've heard it commented. And yet"—he tapped his chest with his index finger—"we are much different here. The heart, the seat of bravery, is empty in you."

Soulai winced as if he'd been slapped. Then he set his jaw. "Why did you call me here?"

"To see about Ti."

"You could have come to the stable," Soulai said evenly, "and seen him for yourself. It's been over two weeks."

Habasle looked away. "Not done as easily as it is said." He turned back with a crazed grin. "You see, someone is trying to, shall we say, clip my wings?"

Just one? Soulai thought grimly.

"It's because I'll be king after Ashurbanipal."

Soulai remembered the ashipu's mocking words. Again his thoughts must have shown on his face, for Habasle spoke vehemently. "I wouldn't place too much faith in the idle chatter of washerwomen," he said. "I am what I say I am, and what I will be. Now, how soon can Ti be ridden?"

Soulai couldn't rein in his emotions any longer. "He's useless to you," he declared. "The head charioteer says he's ruined. He said you took him on the lion hunt too soon, that it stole his courage."

"He'll find it again," Habasle said. "He has to."

"Why does he have to?"

"The mark of Ninurta. It's his destiny to be a great horse—courageous in hunt, brave in battle."

"Even if that means being killed in battle?"

"What more glorious destiny? As long as you take the lives of two or more enemies first—at least you've improved the odds. As Enlil is my witness, do they breed boys without spines in your mountains?"

Again Soulai felt as if he'd been struck. The words could have come straight from his father. His shoulders heaved and he didn't hear the next question until it was repeated.

"I said, do you know the month of your birth?"

Soulai glared. "Adar."

"Aha! The fishes. Do you know which day?"

Soulai shook his head.

"I've just been learning something new about the stars, something they're studying in another land. And I'll bet a whole shekel that when you were born the stars of Pisces were overhead. Which means that as one of the two fishes, you have a choice: to swim upstream—harder, but quite often more rewarding—or downstream, much like a twig at the river's whims."

"I don't swim," Soulai started to say, but his words were drowned by the shriek of another's.

"What is this filthy stable boy doing in the royal library?"

The ashipu was blocking the entrance to the narrow room, cutting off what little light filtered in. Soulai cowered as Habasle pushed himself up to a standing position. The tall man walked toward them, flicking his long fingers in the manner of chasing away a bother-some insect. "He is not educated," he said. "And he leaves his work unfinished. Be off with you. Now."

Though he wanted nothing more at that moment than to flee the library, Soulai was held in place by a firm "No." With his heart pounding, he watched Habasle look directly into the ashipu's searing eyes and say, "He stays. I have summoned him to ask about the health of my horse, the parti-color you were ordered to save."

"And?"

They both turned to Soulai.

"Sssssss!" the ashipu hissed, lifting his hand in the air as if to strike. Soulai cringed. "Come, come, boy. What do you say? How fares the beast?"

"Better," Soulai croaked. "He's a little better." He didn't miss the look of relief that smoothed the ashipu's domed forehead. "I grazed him yesterday—the first day he's been out. He's eating more, but . . ." He paused, glancing between the two.

"But what?" the ashipu prompted.

"The head charioteer says he's ruined." He fidgeted a little. For some reason he didn't take pleasure in laying blame upon Habasle in front of this evil-looking man.

Still, no emotion registered on Habasle's face. "How

many days have passed since the ashipu treated him?" he asked.

After counting on his fingers, Soulai answered, "Sixteen."

Habasle squared his shoulders and lifted his chin. "Sixteen days have passed since your treatment and my horse has not returned to health. Why have the demons lingered so long in his body?"

The ashipu's brow furrowed. "It is not your place to ask about demons!" he shouted. "What do you know about demons?" His breath caught in a faint gasp as an idea appeared to come to him, and the scowl melted away. "Perhaps these are more demanding demons than I realized," he said in a suddenly smooth voice. "Perhaps they require a sacrifice. A royally bred stallion might appease them."

Soulai felt the blood drain from his cheeks. He glanced at Habasle, who was paler as well.

"You're bluffing," Habasle stammered. "What my horse needs is attention to his wounds. Perhaps—"

The ashipu's eyes sparked. "Perhaps," he interrupted, "perhaps I should turn my attention to you. For you, too, I have come to understand, need attention to your wounds." The corners of his mouth twisted upward.

For the first time, a shot of undisguised fear flashed through Habasle's eyes. "No, I am healing," he said.

The ashipu stretched out his arm. As if by sorcery it seemed to grow longer and longer until the curling nails of his fingers closed on Habasle's shoulder. He smiled a wicked smile. "The king, in whose image the gods direct us, has ordered it. And one doesn't deny a god, does one? You will come with me."

TO CAPTURE 9 THE STARS

Soulai stood motionless in the unlit room until the footsteps of Habasle and the ashipu had faded. Only then did he try to make his way out. His uncertain steps through the library's maze of rooms attracted the attention of one of the young scribes, who quickly led him back to the entrance. Delivered into the intense heat, Soulai stood squinting beneath the harsh light of midday. After a moment he noticed that Naboushoumidin, still clutching the leash of the mastiff, appeared to be waiting for him. The man nodded as he stepped from the shadow of one of the winged bulls.

"We are headed in the same direction, no?" he asked in his bright manner. The mastiff suddenly lunged after a turtledove, nearly pulling the old scribe off his feet. Several jerks on the leash hauled the huge animal back in line. When the three were again headed to the south side of the palace, Naboushoumidin cast a sidelong glance and said, "You've not been a slave long, have you?"

Soulai, surprised, shook his head.

"How did he know? you are thinking." Naboushoumidin chuckled. "You see, you are yet wearing that . . . um . . . unsettled expression. You are one foot here, one foot there," he said, hopping from his left to his right. "I mean to say, you *want* to be elsewhere . . . but you *must* be here."

Soulai felt his head moving up and down.

"I remember how it was," Naboushoumidin went on. "I was already a young man—seventeen—when my city was captured. Because I had been taught the letters, and could read and speak three languages, I was shelved in the library." He jerked a thumb over his shoulder. "Oh, it wasn't much then. King Esarhaddon, who came before, only wanted his legacy to be conquering the pyramids. But King Ashurbanipal, now there's a scholar. He demands the texts owned by every city he captures. And my work is to copy each and every one of them for the palace collection: lists of omens, incantations for illnesses, puffed-up tales of triumph told over and over." He heaved an exaggerated sigh. "Endless work, endless! When I was younger I imagined I would simply stop breathing from the awfulness of it all. Even tried it." Pulling the dog to a halt, Naboushoumidin drew in his breath and puffed out his cheeks. His gray head bobbled as his eyes bulged. Passersby nudged their neighbors and traded smiles. Soulai began to grow nervous. Then the scribe let out his breath in a gush and grinned from ear to ear. "Still can't put myself out of my own misery." He slapped his chest. "This old body wants to see a few more days." He shrugged. "Many suns have set; the bones of Esarhaddon, and Sennacherib before him, and Sargon the Second before him, are dust. And King Ashurbanipal's library bursts with 268,492 tablets—now being patiently copied by my assistants. These tablets will outlive us all. So how does a man measure his worth?"

"By his scars, according to my father," Soulai grumbled.

Naboushoumidin cocked his head. "That is the view of a blind man. Was your city captured as well?"

"No. He . . . sold me."

"Ah." The scribe paused and asked gently, "Some misfortune . . . ?"

Soulai described the fire and the debt owed Jahdunlim. The scribe listened intently, then asked, "And your name?"

"Soulai."

"Well, Soulai, what is your position here that you wear the face of an old man?"

"Stable boy. I take care of ten horses."

"And you do not like these horses?"

"Oh, no! I do! I love everything about them: the way their breath smells like honey after they've had their grain, and the way their forelocks fall in fringes across their eyes—I used to put that into my sculptures. And then there's this one stallion—" Soulai cut himself short, blushing.

"Hmmm. You speak as an artist. Perhaps you are misplaced." Naboushoumidin looked thoughtful. "So it's not the horses. Must be Habasle then."

Soulai's head jerked up. "How did you know?"

The scribe chuckled. "'Fierce heart against fierce heart,'" he quoted. "The Epic of Gilgamesh?" He raised his eyebrows questioningly, but Soulai's blank expression showed no recognition. "No matter. There are, perhaps, more persons in this palace who dislike Habasle than I have tablets in my library. But I do not find him so intolerable—his dogs, maybe"—he wrinkled his nose in the direction of the mastiff—"but Habasle—he's just another prince in a long line of princes." The man snaked his hand through the air in the manner of endless waves upon the ocean.

Soulai frowned. "Habasle says he'll be king."

His statement was met with a snort. "If I could fasten a harness around the might that Habasle puts into his dreaming," the scribe said, "I could pull the moon from the night sky. He is much like the king in the story, no?"

Again Soulai wore a blank face.

"Aagh! So much lacking in your education. Come over here. Sit a moment in the shade of this tree."

"But Mousidnou will—"

"Work can always wait, for there is always more work. I am chief scribe to King Ashurbanipal; I will speak on your behalf. Let's see now . . ." Lifting a foot precariously high in the air, he cautiously placed it on the mastiff's haunches. The huge animal looked around and, with noticeable disdain, sat. Naboushoumidin settled himself on the low wall surrounding the tree and, resting his sandaled feet lightly atop the mastiff's back, allowed himself a small grin of triumph.

Soulai, respectful of the man's years, sat cross-legged on the tiles, though a wary distance from the dog.

"Now listen to my words," Naboushoumidin began. "Long ago, in a land not far from here, there lived a young king who wanted more than anything to throw a rope around the great horse of stars in the night sky that he might have it for his own. So he called in his advisers and demanded that they come up with a way for him to reach the sky.

"'You could build a giant ladder,' said one.

"'In all of my land there isn't enough wood for that,' argued the king.

"'You could climb our highest tower and shoot arrows at it,' said another.

"'I want to capture the horse, not kill it,' sneered the king.

"'You could harness birds to a basket and be flown up into the sky,' offered a young adviser who was always thinking.

"'I like it!' said the king. 'I order you to gather one thousand birds.'

"So a call was put out and all across the land people began snaring birds and bringing them to the palace. Strings were knotted, one end around each bird's leg and the other end to the basket, until there were a thousand birds affixed. Finally, when dusk fell and the stars began twinkling, the king climbed into the basket.

"'I'm ready!' he cried.

"But the birds, being ravens and doves and plovers, all day-flying birds, slept. The king was furious. He climbed out of the basket and shouted at his young adviser.

"'Get me some night-flying birds and have this basket ready tomorrow or I'll have you thrown down a well,' he threatened.

"So the next morning another call was put out, and

this time, from all across the land, people began gathering bats. As it was daylight, the winged creatures were fast asleep and had no idea that they were being harnessed to a basket. The king was very pleased, and, just as the sun was setting, he climbed into the basket and stared at the sky, waiting for his horse of stars to appear.

"The young adviser appeared at his side. 'This could be dangerous,' he warned the king. 'Perhaps we should attach a long rope to the basket—'

"'So you can pull me to the ground and keep me away from my horse?' the king cried. 'I won't hear of any such thing.'

"The sun set as he finished speaking and the bats began to stir. Alarmed to find themselves tethered, they unfolded their wings at once and flew into the sky like a great black cloud. The king in his basket was carried along with them, higher and higher and looking smaller and smaller, until he was no bigger than one eye on his great horse of stars."

Naboushoumidin looked at Soulai and grinned. "I can't tell you what became of him, but I can say that since that day no king has tried to capture the stars."

Soulai shared the scribe's amusement. "Have you told that story to Habasle?"

"I could tell it, but the question is, would he hear it?"

Naboushoumidin swatted a fly away from his face. "He may one day be king, but you must be the young adviser. Always thinking, no?" He tapped his forehead with his finger.

By this time the mastiff had stretched out, his massive head resting on his paws. His shoulders vibrated with rapid breathing. More flies clustered around the moist rims of his closed eyes. Naboushoumidin rose stiffly, tugged on the leash, and the dog sleepily stood up. The three continued across the courtyard.

Just before they reached the stable, Naboushoumidin spoke. "I have been guessing, Soulai, ever since I saw you at the library's entrance, that you have a question. I have all the knowledge of all the lands at my fingertips. So what is it that most troubles your heart?"

Soulai thought about himself, about the years of slavery awaiting him. Images crashed through his mind; images of his father grabbing his wrists, of his mother crying, of Soulassa—was she a wife already? He remembered her gathering up the stiff-legged horses he had molded from clay. And then he thought of Ti. The dull coat, the lifeless eyes. More than anything else he wanted to know if Ti would ever get better, if he'd get back his spirit. If, somehow, he, Soulai, would be able to—

"What?" the scribe prompted.

"Ti," Soulai whispered. "Do you know what will happen to Ti?"

"Who is this Ti?"

"A horse . . . the most incredible horse you could ever . . ." Soulai's voice trailed off. How could he fit words around the stallion's spirit, a fire he had once sensed but could not see? Suddenly uncomfortable, Soulai bowed his head and turned toward the stable.

"Wait," Naboushoumidin said and Soulai halted as if under a spell. "This horse, I see now, he is one with you. Perhaps it is his troubled spirit that is showing itself in your eyes. How is he in danger?"

Soulai turned around, the emotions rising within him. He told Naboushoumidin everything about Ti, how the mark of Ninurta forecast a glorious future, how Habasle had nearly killed him during the lion hunt, how the horse seemed to have lost his spirit, and how Habasle was demanding Ti's return so that he could ride him into battle, possibly to be killed for real.

The scribe frowned and drew back. "Are you more worried for Ti or for yourself?"

"For Ti, of course." Soulai was surprised. Didn't the man understand that Ti might die?

"Because he might die," Naboushoumidin said.

The words echoed his thoughts so exactly that a shiver ran through Soulai as he nodded.

"But you have said this horse's destiny is watched over by Ninurta, god of the hunt and god of war. Death is inescapable in both."

Soulai stared at the gray-haired scribe.

"Listen to me. Each one of us has a destiny that must be pursued wholeheartedly, yea though it brings death early, for death will surely come eventually. 'Year upon year the river swells past its banks; the butterfly lives but a day.' Gilgamesh again. You should read it sometime. You see, animals, people, even kings—they're born and they die. The truly great ones will have their deeds recorded in the tablets and chiseled onto the palace walls, so that they may inspire those who follow. Don't let your own soft heart cheat this horse of his rightful destiny."

Soulai felt tears welling in his eyes. His only response was to spin and race for the stable, leap down the stairs and tumble into its comforting dusk. Suddenly it seemed that everyone expected Ti to die. Well, he wasn't going to let that happen. He sprinted down the aisle, ignoring the complaints of his leg, skidded around the corner, and rushed to Ti's side.

The horse startled and pulled back on his tether. Soulai boldly threw his arms around Ti's upper neck and let the sobs come. Through his misery, he felt the stallion touch his shoulder, gently nuzzling him, offering a comfort that only doubled Soulai's determination to guard his friend.

GALLOP WITHOUT WARNING

Soulai's vow of protection doubled his work pace. So worried was he to be apart from Ti now that he trotted the other horses out to the watering trough, fidgeted while they skimmed the rippling surface with their lips, then hurriedly returned them to the stable. And even though the month of Elul continued to burn with the heat of the kilns, he jogged from task to task: flinging manure, raking bedding, running horses to and from the armory.

The wound in Ti's neck finally healed, and Soulai began slicking the stallion's hide with his hands and his spit until the fine hairs gleamed. But try as he might, he couldn't smooth away the scars. Their defiant ugliness marred Ti's beauty the way the fire's snaking cracks had scarred his clay horses. The scars implied that the gold and white stallion was imperfect—tested and found wanting. Soulai reminded himself that Ti's scars were the lion's fault, or, rather, Habasle's. He rubbed cedar oil into the thickened skin and polished Ti's arching neck, all the while staring into the pale blue eye that yet spoke nothing.

He had to help Ti recover his courage, Soulai decided, but in the next instant he just as vehemently changed his mind. No, no, he didn't have to. If Ti remained timid, no one would ask anything of him. Habasle would forget the stallion and there would be no lions to face, no wars to join.

The unresolved worry drew him to Ti's side day and night until Soulai gave up and began sleeping in the stable. To feed himself he begged from the kitchens a roasted ear of corn or a duck egg, or he stole from an unattended basket a handful of almonds. Sitting in the darkness, then, he watched and chewed and contemplated. To his surprise he noticed that the forearms resting atop his knees were now banded with muscles. And a finger to his ribs showed that despite the little food he was eating, he had actually grown larger. A wave of pride in his manliness surged through him before self-consciousness chased it away.

Over the next several weeks, in the quiet of the night, Soulai became a part of the stable's private world. He was surprised to learn that it was a world in which the inhabitants slept very little. A few horses dozed off and on in the powdered manure, but most stood throughout the night, swishing their tails and nickering to each other. An occasional squeal spoke insult, a snap of the teeth, retort.

Soulai discovered other inhabitants of the stable: bats living beneath the high thatched roof. He watched with keen interest as they unfolded nightly from their upside-down sleep and winged out of the stable entry. For some reason, one bat kept returning throughout the night. After several nights Soulai made out the tiny pink shape of a baby bat plastered to the rafters, and this became the first place Soulai looked each evening. He began counting the number of trips the mother made, usually nodding off to sleep after four or five.

One night, after the mother bat had flown off with the now furry baby clinging to her chest, Soulai was lying on a rough cushion of barley hay listening to an unseen horse steadily pawing at the stone floor. The monotonous scraping was lulling Soulai to sleep when he realized that the rhythm had become footsteps. He opened his eyes just enough to make out someone carrying an armload of tack down the aisle. Pretending to be asleep, he kept his eyes slitted, watching, until the person stopped in front of him. Long bronze spurs poked from the backs of heavily tooled sandals. Soulai opened his eyes wider and saw Habasle, with two leather pouches draped across his shoulders, fastening a rug onto Ti's back.

Soulai sat up. "What are you doing?"

Habasle unknotted the tether and slipped a bridle over Ti's ears. "Taking my horse," he said without turning around.

"Where?"

Ti was backing into the aisle. The sharp hooves narrowly missed Soulai's toes as he scrambled to his feet.

"Where are you taking him?" he asked again.

"You ask too many questions for a slave. Get out of my way."

"Wait." Soulai boldly reached for the reins. "Take me, too."

Habasle slapped away the hand. "No! I order you to stay." He began leading Ti toward the starlit opening at the end of the stable. Fear seized Soulai. He stumbled after Habasle. On impulse he dove amid a row of horses and unknotted the tether of a bald-faced chestnut stallion. He hurried him backward, then trotted him all the way to the courtyard.

Habasle was untying the same mastiff he'd had at the library, the one he called Annakum, and to Soulai's surprise, he fussed over the dog as he would a small child. Gently he rubbed each ear between his fingers. Putting a finger to his lips, Habasle offered Annakum a treat. The moment was interrupted by Ti squealing a challenge and the chestnut answering it. Habasle immediately straightened. He looked embarrassed, then frowned at Soulai. "This doesn't concern you. Go back to your sleep."

"I'm supposed to take care of your horses," Soulai responded stubbornly, "especially Ti."

But Habasle, juggling the mastiff's collar and a spear in one hand, and Ti's reins in the other, began walking away. Soulai took a deep breath, looked over both shoulders and up at the blue-black sky. A brilliant star chanced to arc through the void like a hurled spear. When it disappeared, Soulai bit his lip and set off after Habasle.

What are we doing? he wondered. Going on a hunt—in the middle of the night? He looked at the chestnut stallion pacing alertly at his side. And why, of all horses, did I untie this one? Ti hates him.

Soulai grimaced as he recalled the day when the two stallions, tethered side by side, had suddenly pinned back their ears and begun kicking. Wicked screams had punctuated the sickening thuds of hooves into flesh as stable boys ran from all directions. At Soulai's begging, Mousidnou had let Ti stay; the chestnut was exchanged for a mousy roan.

If only I'd decided to follow sooner, he thought, I could be leading that roan. He shook his head as a distinct uneasiness tickled his belly. I don't have a rug; I don't even have a bridle. If Habasle is planning one of his hunts—as the mastiff and spear seem to indicate—I may as well jump headfirst into the lion's mouth.

But instead of leaving the stable courtyard and the palace by the curving ramp, Habasle headed in the opposite direction. He led Ti up the limestone steps to an adjoining courtyard, turned, and walked up another set of steps. The horses slipped and scrambled over the uneven ground and Soulai was certain that their clattering hooves would alert a guard. But none approached, and soon they were making their way through the kitchen's shadows and past the glowing mouths of the kilns. Bakers working through the night lifted their heads to watch indifferently before returning to their paddles and fragrant loaves.

The next courtyard was nothing more than bare dirt littered with broken urns, empty baskets, haphazard stacks of bagged grain, and more than one lopsided cart missing a wheel. Although darkness enveloped them, Soulai could see Habasle looking nervously left and right.

"What're you huntin' at this hour?"

The gruff voice came from nowhere. Soulai jumped.

"Whatever's awake," Habasle casually answered the guard at a small gate that was nearly hidden by baskets of stinking trash. The man touched his hand to the hilt of his sheathed knife but stepped aside as Habasle pulled on the door and guided first Annakum and then Ti through the narrow opening. The lintel was set so low that the stallion had to duck his head. When Soulai followed, the guard stepped forward, and for a moment Soulai thought he was going to stop him. But the man just looked him up and down, belched, and squatted on the ground, scratching his stomach.

The stench of rotting garbage that had been dumped outside the palace wall assaulted his nostrils as he followed Habasle north. A skinny yellow dog scuttled away from an overturned basket, but otherwise the city lay still. At the palace's northeast corner, Habasle paused. He peered into the darkness. The horses stopped, stamped, then suddenly pricked their ears in unison. Soulai shivered; something was waiting around the corner. He held his breath and listened. He heard nothing, but gradually, a reddish shape moved closer until he could see that it was the ashipu himself standing in their path. The tall man confidently reached out and closed his fingers around Ti's reins.

"Hunting bats?"

Annakum growled, long and low.

"Or showing yourself to be one?" The man's throaty chuckle held no mirth. "Come—squeak, squeak, boy—like the frightened creature of the night that you are."

Habasle stiffened but remained silent.

"You're a waste of my time," the ashipu sneered. "The silver hardly warrants . . . Give!" He tried to pull the reins from Habasle's hand. Ti grunted at the blow to his tender mouth.

"Take your hands off my horse." The words came quietly, but loaded with warning.

The ashipu jerked the reins again. Ti's pained squeal was followed by him heaving his weight left, then right, trying to escape the cruel pressure on his bridle.

"*Your* horse." The ashipu spat. "You insolent cur. He's been royally bred for royalty only. And now I've chosen him for sacrifice."

"If you try to harm this horse, I'll cut out your heart and feed it to you."

Soulai, creeping closer, saw the ashipu's black eyes narrow. The man drew himself up. Summoning his evil powers, Soulai thought. The night air seemed to grow strangely thin and Soulai could scarcely breathe.

"Your ill manners profess your ill breeding." Light from the half-moon glinted on the blade of a knife pulled from the ashipu's robe. In one quick motion he grasped Ti's headstall and laid the silvery blade against the white throat. Ti snorted but stood as still as stone, as if under a spell. Even Annakum, who had kept up a steady growl, fell silent.

Habasle immediately dropped the reins, which swung noiselessly in the darkness. He took one retreating step, then another. He switched his spear to his right hand, calmly leveled it to his waist, and eyed the distance to the ashipu's belly.

The red-robed man smiled. Still staring at Habasle, he slowly drew the knife across Ti's hide so that a dark trickle spread through the hairs. He shook his head. "Not a wise choice, little bat. Now put it down."

Habasle hesitated. Then he turned and defiantly hurled the spear into the night. No one spoke until they heard it clank to the ground.

The smile never left the ashipu's face. "You," he said to Habasle, "and you," indicating Soulai, "are going to assist me in a much-needed cleansing ritual."

But as the ashipu had drawn his knife, Soulai had begun creeping around to the chestnut's other side. He hoped they wouldn't notice him leaning his body into the horse. The pressure signaled the stallion to step toward Ti. Ears twitched. Muscles tightened. Soulai held his breath and leaned again. The chestnut swung his hip forcefully around this time, bumping against Ti. The old feud was rekindled and the parti-color stallion lashed out with both hooves. Humping his back, the chestnut returned the blows, kicking again and again. Ti bellowed and spun sideways, and the knife fell from the ashipu's hand.

Encumbered by his long robe, the man tried to evade the flailing hooves of the fighting stallions while searching for the lost dagger. Just as he found it, however, Annakum's jaws clamped onto his naked wrist. The huge dog shook his head and the man crumpled, shrieking in pain.

Habasle grabbed Ti's reins and yanked him away from the fight. In one leap he was on the stallion's back and drumming his legs along his flanks. They sped toward the city's walls.

Soulai yanked sharply on the lead rope of the angry chestnut. In desperation, he jumped for the horse's back, managing to get only one knee locked over the withers before the animal bolted. The rope fell from his hands. All too aware of the rough ground rushing beneath him, Soulai grabbed for the mane and tried to pull himself upright. With a final, all-out effort he heaved his body atop the galloping stallion, crouched low, and ordered his quivering legs to squeeze tight.

One of Nineveh's main entrances, the Nergal Gate, lay directly ahead, but Habasle steered Ti toward a smaller one, which had a door standing ajar and a lone guard waiting nervously beside it. Having neither reins nor lead rope, Soulai felt lucky that his galloping mount veered in the same direction. Ti and Habasle rushed into the tunnel that pierced the thick inner wall. The chestnut charged after, bashing Soulai's leg against the bricks. In a couple of strides they were passing through a twin gate in the city's towering outer wall. His entire leg took the blow this time. There was no pausing to notice the shattering pain, for the stallion suddenly bunched and sprang through the darkness over a liquid black moat. They landed hard on the opposite side and Soulai struggled to balance as the horse scrambled. And then they were galloping again, Soulai lurching precariously with each stride, the horse's spine splitting him with each footfall. Blinded by his wind-whipped tears, he gasped when the chestnut lunged into the air again, grunted when they crashed to ground on the far side of another moat. The coarse hairs of the mane cut into his fingers, but he refused to let go. In the span of a dozen wild heartbeats, they were away from Nineveh, thundering headlong into the blackness of the unknown.

PART 2

A sickness coursed through the bat's veins. He had to struggle just to keep his balance on the edge of the palace watering trough. Over the stable's manure piles his cousins clouded the night air, swooping low to pick off dung beetles and spiders and carry them to the thatched rooftop to be swallowed. But the young bat couldn't swallow. He could barely perch, his body swaying from side to side, his mouth agape. Confusion pounded in his head.

That dog had just come through the courtyard, the same one that he'd bitten . . . when was it? Through his mind's haze he recalled the night when the huge dog had surprised him, had knocked him from the trough to the floor. When the black nose sniffed close, he'd sunk his teeth into it. That had prompted a loud yelp, and, while the dog circled, rubbing at his nose with a paw, he'd managed to right himself and finally to fly off to a low wall.

He couldn't remember when that was now. The moon was always waxing and waning, no end. His head throbbed harder. He shook it, trying to dispel the cloudiness. The movement unbalanced him. Instinctively he spread his wings, but already he was falling.

A small splash, heard by no one, and water enveloped him. The cold liquid shrouded his weak struggle, gradually suppressed his breathing, then cradled his lifeless body for the remainder of the night.

THE URIDIMMU

Sunlight warmed Soulai's face, nudging him awake. He rolled onto his back, stretched, and yawned. For a few moments he relished the luxury of uninterrupted quiet. Then memories of the previous night began charging through his mind. He opened his eyes and was struck by a sapphire sky so immense that he instantly felt small and insignificant. Where am I? he wondered. Curling onto his side again, wincing at the newly aroused aches in his legs and hips, he surveyed the area.

Habasle sat a short distance away, his back to Soulai. He seemed to be talking to Annakum, even leaning over to brush his cheek along the dog's head. Annakum returned the caress with a sloppy lick, and, smiling, Habasle offered the dog a tidbit—a dried fig, it looked like. Then he popped one into his own mouth and shifted his position. Soulai saw now that Habasle had a small white rock in his hand, which he began striking against the flat face of a boulder. He was hunched to the right; the spear wound obviously still troubled him.

Soulai stretched again, and this time his movement attracted Annakum's attention. Although the mastiff remained prone, he studied Soulai intently with cold eyes the color of pale moons. Soulai scarcely breathed. He didn't so much as twitch until he became aware of shadows on either side of him. Glancing over his shoulder and squinting into the sun's glare, he discovered two bearded vultures on the rocky crest at his back. Their enormous sooty wings hung open like charred palm fronds. Just like Annakum, they watched him. But there was something more in their gaze, Soulai realized; there was a patient hunger, a confident expectance of death—his death!

He jumped to his feet. That brought Annakum to his, a long growl rumbling from his throat. Soulai tensed. He wanted to run, but wasn't sure how far a stumbling flight would take him before the dog's fangs or the vultures' bony wings knocked him to the ground.

He shifted his gaze from the shaggy-headed birds to the snarling dog and back again. A fist-sized rock lay within reach, and, keeping a wary eye on Annakum, he cautiously bent to pick it up. The sharp weight in his hand made him feel better and he stood taller. The mastiff quit growling but shot a threatening glance in

Soulai's direction. Then, padding a tight circle, he flopped beside his master.

Habasle had ignored the standoff, so Soulai broke the silence. "Where are we?" he asked. The words came croaking from his dry throat, sounding more fearful than he would have liked. But the noise was enough to discourage the scavengers. One vulture flapped its wings and lifted itself into the air. After a clumsy bit of hopping, the other bird followed.

"North of the city," Habasle answered while continuing to draw. "Near a road leading to Harran. Or to Dur Sharrukin."

Soulai sidled toward the line of boulders that partially ringed their encampment. In the distance, Nineveh's sharp-toothed outer wall glinted in the morning sun. He could see the Khosr River flowing from the city and separating into brown ribbons that filled the moats and canals. Spotting movement atop the walls, he could have sworn that guards pointed in their direction.

A strange feeling crept over him. Three months ago, when he was being led toward this city, his heart had pounded with fear; now that he stood outside it, he had an irrational longing to return to it.

His thoughts were interrupted by a rustling in the underbrush. The horses! At least he was still with Ti; he could still protect him. Annakum pricked his ears, but only followed with his eyes as Soulai warily left the clearing.

A wadi, as deep as a man is tall, and thick with feathery grasses and date palms, lay behind them, and it was there that Habasle and Soulai had hidden the two horses last night. But when Soulai made it to the bank, he found only one horse. He shook his head and sighed. He had expected it, really, for Habasle had ridden from the palace with hobbles tucked inside his pouch, and so Ti still shuffled along the streambed, tugging at stalks with his teeth. The lead rope, which was all Soulai had had to knot around the ankles of the bald-faced chestnut, lay empty atop some crushed grasses.

Ti heard Soulai's approach and whinnied. It was the familiar morning greeting that signaled hunger, and Soulai hated not having some grain to feed him. As he picked his way down the crumbling dirt walls, he watched the gold-and-white stallion wade through the sea of plumes like some magical mount belonging to Ea, the water god.

When they met, Soulai extended his hand. Ti stretched his neck to lick the salty palm, sucked and slobbered, all the while gazing at Soulai with gratitude. Soulai smiled. Until he saw the dried blood on the stallion's throat. He remembered with horror that the ashipu still wanted to kill Ti. That Habasle wanted to ride him into battle. How am I going to protect him? he wondered. Especially out here, in the middle of nowhere, and on foot.

He sighed again. Ti stopped his licking to rub his head against Soulai's shoulder. Soulai smiled and helped scratch the sweat-stiffened hairs left by the bridle. He had been worried that last night's hard gallop would drain the recuperating horse, but instead it appeared to have invigorated him. Even hobbled, Ti moved with more ease than he had since the lion hunt.

He continued scratching the horse, flaking away the dried lather on his chest and belly. The white marking of the winged creature, Ninurta's mark as everyone called it, caught his attention. Slowly he traced his fingers along the outline. Was Ti really destined to go to war? The words of Naboushoumidin, the chief scribe, came back to him: *Animals, people, even kings— they're born and they die. . . . Don't let your own soft heart cheat this horse of his rightful destiny.* Soulai clenched his teeth. No. He couldn't let Ti be killed.

When his fingers finally tired, he patted the stallion on the neck, picked up the empty lead rope, and climbed out of the wadi.

"We've lost a horse," he announced as he entered the encampment.

Habasle was still busy at the rock. "No," he responded,

"*you've* lost a horse. Mine's where I left him." He jerked a finger over his shoulder.

Soulai glared. He's already forgotten how I helped him escape the ashipu last night, he thought bitterly. The skin beneath his brand twitched. He was a mere slave, a tool, something to be used and discarded. Just like Ti. He squinted at the vultures circling overhead and vowed not to speak further.

The sun climbed higher, shadows shortened, and the rocky ground began to burn through his sandals. Only his growling stomach interrupted the quiet in the clearing. But Habasle, who had switched from the figs to a crusty round of emmer bread, didn't offer to share.

It was sometime later that the noisy approach of something large startled both boys. Soulai caught his breath and heard Habasle do the same, until Ti shuffled into the encampment and they both relaxed, trying to hide their relief. The horse was all curiosity, nostrils flaring, ears swiveling. He sniffed at the rumpled rug, then at the pouch sitting beside it. When he smelled the lead rope that had been used to hobble the chestnut stallion, he squealed and stamped his front hooves on it. Soulai smiled.

He'd been watching Habasle's work for the better part of the morning now. White lines nearly covered the boulder's surface, and they were beginning to resemble a battle scene. Boredom combined with curiosity over-came his vow. "What are you doing?" he asked at last.

"Making my mark," came the reply. The steady clacking sound of rock hitting rock continued.

"Why?"

"So they'll know I was here."

"Who?"

"Whoever, or whatever, is following us."

A chill ran along Soulai's sweaty neck. He remembered the ashipu. Instinctively he glanced toward Nineveh. "What do you mean?"

Habasle turned around. Soulai was astonished to see how much fresh blood had soaked the tunic. Habasle's eyes shone dark and feverish; his words tumbled over one another. "I mean that the ashipu saw it, too. All the month of Sebat the three stars on the true shepherd's belt twinkled, meaning the wings of Ninurta would brush the shoulder of the next king. But while everyone was searching the skies, I found the god's own image on Ti. And on me." He pressed two fingers across the tattoo on his upper arm.

Soulai ignored the claims. "So who's following us?"

Habasle reached for the pouch nearest him. The effort made him groan and clutch his side, but he dragged it over, pulled something out, and tossed it.

A polished stone object landed in Soulai's palm. His

fingers opened to reveal a strange creature, half man and half animal, carved from lapis lazuli. Different from a lamassu, this one had hairy legs, upon which sat the torso of a bearded man; the arms were raised to invoke a prayer—or a curse.

"What is it?"

Habasle sank back against the boulder, still cupping his side. "An uridimmu. A mad lion or mad dog, depending on the curse. But it's meant for us."

Sweat dampened Soulai's palm. "This is what's following us?"

"If the ashipu's powers are strong enough. And they must be, for it appeared in my pouch without my knowledge."

"And you're marking this rock to help it find us?"

"Yes," he said. "I want it, the ashipu—I want all of them to find us. I want the whole world to know that I, Habasle, son of Ashurbanipal, king of the universe, king of Assyria, for whom Ashur, king of the gods, and Ishtar, lady of battle, have decreed a destiny of heroism, stood here on this day."

The words, bloated with ego or fever, charged through the midmorning stillness. Soulai looked over his shoulder again. Then over the other one. "Shouldn't we be riding on then?"

There was no answer, only Annakum's rapid panting

and then the steady clack-clack of Habasle returning to his drawing. Soulai bit his lip. A small panic told him to run far away from the image that seemed to burn like fire in his hand. He dropped the carved blue stone onto the crumpled pouch. The feeling of being small and insignificant returned. He crossed his arms and paced circles. Annakum lifted his head, visibly annoyed, so he stopped. Then he stood watching Habasle. "What are you drawing?" he asked at last.

"Me. On Ti. Look, I'm spearing a Mede. See? Piercing him straight through his middle. And there's another I've already slain behind me."

This time Soulai chose not to respond. Habasle twisted around. "Don't you see it?"

A frown wrinkled Soulai's forehead.

"So be it," Habasle said, handing him the white stone. "You do better."

Soulai sighed and, still frowning, sat down. A rotten odor arose from Habasle's clothing, along with a moist heat. But at least this was something to do, and, after studying Ti a moment, Soulai bent into the boulder. Thick, confident lines began filling its surface. He thought about the little clay horses he had formed in his hands and rounded his marks with their fullness. He remembered the incredible power of last night's ride and drew Ti's barrel lean, the legs stretched long.

Habasle's attentive silence signaled approval. Somewhat reluctantly Soulai finished drawing his master on Ti's back and filled in the dying Mede beneath Ti's pounding hooves. Then, thinking back on the chiseled panels he had studied outside the library, he added a feathered headdress to Ti's bridle and fastened fat tassels from his throatlatch and breast-collar. The horse's noble image appeared poised to leap from the boulder.

For a while, Habasle just sat at his side, staring. A smile played about his lips. Then he began to nod. "Yes," he murmured. "Yes. That's exactly how it will look." His burning eyes settled upon Soulai. "Draw yourself, too." He tapped the boulder.

Soulai's mouth hung open. "Why?"

"Because you are my slave!" The abrupt order shattered the brief accord. "Just do it," Habasle said in a calmer voice. "Draw yourself carrying my arrows and a spare shield." He winced; the pain seemed to frighten him. "Listen," he added, "I didn't invite you along last night, but you followed anyway. So you're in the thick of it now, with Ti and me."

Again Soulai bent into the boulder, but the passion had evaporated. The figure he drew looked small and stiff compared with the other images. He set down the white rock.

"Why does the ashipu want to kill you?"

Habasle chewed on a hangnail and shrugged. "Someone's mother has crossed his palm with silver."

"Someone's mother?"

"The mother of a potential king. I have found that not many of Ashurbanipal's sons live to greet their own father. Sillaja, my good friend and brother, laid down after breakfast with a fire in his stomach and never awoke. Irsisi carried a message to the ashipu and never returned, though that son of a jackal declares my brother never arrived."

"But why should he try to kill you? Would he be king then?"

Habasle laced his fingers and loudly cracked his knuckles. "No, but if he has a hand in choosing the next king, he'll find a way to hold the reins."

Soulai could barely speak the next words. "Why does he want to kill Ti?"

"That's my doing. The man owns no interest in horses, probably never even set foot in a stable until I asked him to tend to Ti's injuries. I didn't think he'd notice the markings, but he did—or the asu did. Now, having found Ninurta's omen, he knows that Ti and I together are destined for greatness, so if he can't kill me, he'll kill him—in the name of ritual sacrifice, of course."

A shiver traveled up Soulai's spine as he gazed at the gold-and-white stallion. "What are we going to do?"

The way Habasle kept chewing on his thumbnail while staring at the horizon made Soulai nervous. "What are we going to do?" he repeated urgently. "You have a plan, don't you?"

Habasle's lips spread around his gnawing teeth. "No," he mumbled. He yanked his thumb away. "Well, I plan on living—at least for a time; I just don't know where." He pursed his lips while thinking, and scanned the road below them. Then he looked back toward Nineveh. "Thieves by night," he mused, "jackals, snakes, and now—possibly—mad dogs and lions. Still, there are any number and sorts of enemies in the day, and those more easily seen." He turned to Soulai. "It's about a day's ride to Dur Sharrukin, where we can hide until we make some plans. Would you rather risk the seen or unseen enemy?"

Soulai stared at the fierce blue creature lying on the pouch. "The uridimmu," he asked, "it travels by night?"

Habasle climbed to his feet, suddenly impatient. "I don't know and I don't care. Don't waste your time whining about something you can't control. Now which do you desire?"

Soulai's indignation returned. He stood as well. "What does it matter which I desire? I'm only a slave."

For a moment Habasle looked directly at him. It was a look colored by pity. "And you will always be a slave," he said quietly. "Even when your debt is repaid, you'll still be a slave because you think like a slave." He shaded his eyes and glanced at the sky. "We'll move on until high sun, then rest until nightfall. Fasten the rug on Ti."

RIVER'S EDGE

2

Soulai's stomach growled louder. His feet burned from the hot grit stuck between his toes and from his sandals' chafing straps. But he kept plodding.

The sun was beating straight down on their heads now. Its heat radiated off the stone-strewn road; its light glistened through the long string of saliva dangling from Annakum's black lips. The dog's curling pink tongue fluttered like a heavy-winged butterfly.

Soulai was walking behind and a little to one side of Ti, resting his hand on the sweat-streaked rump. The silvery tail, dulled with dust, switched fitfully. Although the long hairs stung Soulai's shoulders and arms, they provided some relief from the bothersome black gnats that dove at his face, tangling themselves in his eyelashes. Swatting them away for the hundredth time, Soulai shaded his eyes and looked to the road ahead. It shimmered with heat, no end in sight.

Habasle pulled on the reins at that moment and the progression halted. He, too, shaded his eyes and scanned the land, not ahead, but east. Soulai followed his gaze. It took a moment to find the faint trail that sloped away from the road and toward a winding growth of dusty grasses and low trees. Annakum took the opportunity to flop down in the scant shadow of a wormwood bush. His entire body shook with his rapid panting.

Habasle looked down at the dog, then at Soulai. His hand still guarded the lumpy bandage beneath his blood-stained tunic, and he hunched upon Ti's back, blinking, as if trying to steady his thoughts. If he had any, they weren't shared. Abruptly he pulled the reins to the side. Ti stumbled, then dropped his nose to the ground and, blowing little puffs of dust as he went, cautiously began picking his way downhill.

Against a white sky, the two vultures continued gliding in long, looping circles. Why were they so certain death was near? Soulai thought irritably. Heaving a tired sigh, he started down as well. Annakum shook his head violently, climbed to his feet, and followed.

Soulai watched the ground closely, for the path, if you could even call it that, was pitted with exposed rock and creased with fissures. Half a dozen times he slipped on loose pebbles and almost fell.

Before long, brittle-limbed bushes began blocking their way, some taller than Soulai. Even Ti had to stop and start, sometimes doubling back to find a passage. The slight, hot breeze that had seemed an aggravation on the main road evaporated amid the increasingly dense scrub. Sweat streamed down Soulai's back.

Scurrying and fluttering and slithering noises increased as the brush thickened. Soulai was mindful that they weren't the only creatures present, and, with thoughts of the uridimmu consuming him, he flinched. Colorful flocks of darters and bee-eaters waited until the last moment to burst skyward. Red-bellied locusts launched their leathery bodies at his face. At one point, he halted and held his breath as some unseen animal passed nearby. He exhaled with relief when he spotted Annakum weaving his way through the undergrowth. His uneasiness returned, though, when he noticed something unusual in the mastiff's gait. The dog seemed disjointed; he was stumbling over the uneven ground like a drunken man.

Soulai was watching Annakum so intently that a loud grunt dangerously close to his other side caught him by surprise. He spun around in time to get a glimpse of a large, hairy animal pushing its way through the scrub. A boar? Or the uridimmu? He hurried to catch up with Ti.

The stallion moved along more quickly now and Soulai knew why: The cool scent of moisture ahead teased his own nostrils. His dusty throat yearned for a swallow of water, his swollen feet for a soak in a stream. The grasses beneath them turned a brighter green and ceased springing back. Swarms of insects attacked his ankles as a stumpy black and yellow snake glided to cover, leaving a smooth depression in its wake. Hoofprints and footprints began filling with water.

Finally, with the lifting of a palm frond, he could see the river stretched before them, sunlight glinting off its smooth surface. A pair of leggy white egrets waded along the opposite shore. Soulai immediately squatted in the mud and cupped water to his mouth. Ti waded in to his knees, lowered his head and noisily sucked and swallowed, his eyes closed with the sheer pleasure of it. Habasle lifted a leg over the withers and dropped with a small splash. Steadying himself against the horse's shoulder, he gingerly bent and scooped a little water to his mouth. With careful motions he splashed some along his forehead and neck, too.

He stood looking upriver then, and Soulai, turning his head, saw that Annakum, up to his belly in the water, was still panting heavily, but not drinking. The dog seemed confused. Soulai cast a worried look at Habasle, but he, too, wore a blank stare.

Without a word, Habasle turned and laid his hands on Ti's back. He made a little leap to remount, but, apparently, he couldn't summon the strength, for a flick of his wrist summoned Soulai. Although there was no one watching, Soulai flushed with humiliation as he bent his back and Habasle stepped up onto it, then swung his leg over Ti. Habasle gathered the reins and thumped his heels.

Fear grabbed Soulai. Habasle was going to cross the river! And he was taking Ti with him! The opposite shore was only an arrow's flight away, but between the banks stretched a rippling green skin that certainly hid a host of watery monsters.

He wanted to protest and lunge for the reins. But, at Habasle's insistence, the stallion was arching his golden neck and stepping hesitantly deeper and deeper into the river. The thick tail was soon taken up by the current and it floated on the surface like an elegantly fringed veil. Ti's next step apparently found no bottom, for he plunged into the water. The river's force gathered around his body, angling him and his rider downstream.

Soulai's heart pounded so fast he grew dizzy. They were leaving him. How could he follow? He couldn't swim. The current tugged at his calves, taunting him.

He stepped backward, panicking a moment when his sandal got stuck in the mud. He vividly recalled the chiseled stone panel outside the royal library, the one showing people drowning in a river to avoid capture. That's what would happen to him if he dared take even one more step. The waters would grab him and suck him under, squeeze the life from him. Great fishes would nibble at his fingers with their slimy lips. He'd seen it.

Habasle looked over his shoulder and whistled. "Annakum," he called. "Here!"

The mastiff stood still, with his head lolled to one side and two long strings of saliva drooping from his mouth, ignoring his master's summons. Habasle called again; his whistle sounded sharper. The dog pricked his ears but didn't move.

Angered, Habasle yanked Ti's head around and rode the horse the short way back. The current landed them downriver. They came splashing through the shallows, Ti nodding his head and chewing upon the bit as if this were but a game. Annakum jumped aside.

"Annakum, here!" The words pierced the air with authority. Obediently the mastiff rose, waded a few paces, and began swimming the river. The waters pulled him south.

"Do I have to whistle for you, too?" Habasle was rein-ing Ti toward the river.

Soulai fidgeted. "I can't swim."

"Then drown." Heels thudded and Ti stepped off into the current.

Soulai watched them go a second time. His shoulders rose and fell with his rapid breathing. Just let him go, he thought. Let him go. He's sick, wounded—let him die alone. I hope he dies alone. A thought popped into his mind: Then I'll be free! His mind raced. If Habasle died out here in the wilderness, he could take Ti and find his way home, couldn't he?

His stomach doubled upon itself. The fleeting thought of freedom was smothered by fear. He had no idea where he was or how he could possibly survive alone. Maybe the vultures did know the future.

As he watched Ti's gold-and-white head bobbing above the cloudy water, he opened his mouth to beg Habasle to come back. But before there was any sound, the stallion began turning. Ears flattened in annoyance this time, Ti pumped a smooth arc and headed for Soulai.

When his hooves found bottom, the tired horse lugged his dripping body and rider from the water once more. Soulai stared up at the silhouetted pair. Rising as they had from the river's murky underworld, Habasle and Ti appeared regal and godlike.

Between labored breaths Habasle muttered, "I'm not crossing again, so if you're coming, climb on now."

"On Ti?"

"No, on my back. By Ishtar, you're stupid." He sucked in his breath as if a sharp pain had grabbed him. After a moment he slowly let it out. "You helped last night," he said curtly. "I'm helping you now. Climb on."

Soulai threw his arm across Ti's slippery rump and jumped. His chest bumped against the horse's flanks and he slid to the ground. He tried again, grasping the wet rug and jumping higher, but Ti was growing fretful and beginning to prance. A sharp hoof landed on Soulai's toes.

He refused to cry out, for he saw Habasle's scornful expression. A hand was thrust toward him. He gripped it, hopped twice, and leaped as high as he could. Habasle groaned but held steady, and Soulai swung his leg over Ti. The hide was slick; there wasn't much to grab on to. He sat deep, centering his weight over his hips and trying to balance with Ti's ambling gait, for the horse was already heading toward the water.

Across the river Soulai could see Annakum crawling onto the bank. The dog shook off a great halo of spray, then threw himself into a stand of tall grasses, flattening them as he rubbed his coat dry. Soulai hoped he'd live to feel grasses beneath his feet again.

Already the water was lapping at his toes and calves. As it climbed past his knees, he stiffened. He lifted his chin higher, becoming acutely aware of his own breathing. Then Ti stepped into nothingness. Soulai gasped. The horse sank lower; he couldn't hold them both! They were drowning! Cold water rushed between his knees and the warm hide, and he felt his seat lifting from Ti's back. He threw his arms around Habasle's waist and clamped his chin onto his shoulder.

"Ow! Get off me!" Habasle jabbed an elbow backward, but Soulai's grip was frozen. With his free hand, Habasle tugged at one of Soulai's wrists. Strong fingers managed to work it free. Another sharp elbow and Soulai was falling sideways, clawing at Habasle's tunic. Then Soulai tumbled into the river.

The green water closed over his mouth, his nose, his eyes—a suffocating blanket. He gulped a great swallow of muddy water. Flailing, coughing, choking, Soulai reached out blindly. Each tantalizing contact—a flank, Habasle's heel, a hock—slipped from his fingers. Ti was pulling forward, Soulai realized, forward and away, and he was sinking down, drowned and forgotten. As if from a great distance, Soulai watched himself struggle.

Somehow the strands of Ti's long tail drifted between his fingers. They felt as solid as a rope, and he clutched them desperately. Immediately the sinking stopped and Soulai felt himself being towed forward. He twisted, kicking against the water until his face broke through— one quick gasp of air—then sank again below the surface.

Ti's pumping hock caught him in the belly, but Soulai refused to loosen his grip. The horse's stroke grew panicky, but Soulai hung on, gritting his teeth through the pummeling, gasping for air when he could.

At last his toes were dragging through coarse sand. He let go of Ti's tail, managed to bring his feet underneath him, and stood. Clutching his stomach, he coughed uncontrollably. A giant shivering seized him as he fell to his knees. The coughing turned to retching. Smelly water, colored with mud, pushed past his tongue. Out it spilled, from his mouth and his nostrils. He crawled farther up the bank and collapsed face forward.

Behind him he heard Ti's labored breathing. It compressed into a brief grunt as the horse shook himself off, pelting Soulai's back with more water. Then the clanking sound of the iron bit mixed with those of ripping grass and the monotonous twitter of birds. The hot sand warmed Soulai's thighs and arms; it felt good. The sun was blotting dry his skin, the breeze sifting through his hair. He'd live.

Footsteps approached. Soulai opened his eyes to a blurry view of Habasle's feet. Dried figs plopped one after the other onto the sand in front of his nose. Then the feet disappeared.

BEGGARS AND DREAMERS

3

For the third time since they'd left the river, Habasle counted on his fingers and looked over his shoulder. Soulai had turned twice, cringing, expecting to see the uridimmu—in whatever horrible form it took—stalking them. But land and sky, and a sun sinking behind frayed pink clouds, were all he saw. So this time he bent his head and continued trudging up the long, grassy slope. He was exhausted and, to tell the truth, empty of caring. All he wanted was to collapse somewhere and sleep.

As the sun touched the horizon, a quickening wind began flinging dirt and bits of leaves at them. It grew stronger and stronger until both boys had to shield their faces. Ti bent his head into his chest and pushed on. Annakum was nowhere to be seen.

Dur Sharrukin's walls finally loomed ahead and Soulai risked a glance between splayed fingers. The city stretched only half as wide as Nineveh, though a spectacular temple rose from its midst, spiraling in brilliant enameled tiers toward the heavens. The outer walls bristled with nearly half a hundred square towers, their broad stone faces reflecting the orange sun like warriors' shields. He couldn't say exactly what it was, but he sensed there was something odd about this city.

Huge stone slabs began to crop up among the wind-whipped grasses, and first Ti, then Soulai, tripped. Other slabs joined these to form an unkempt roadway to Dur Sharrukin's main gate, but when their footfalls on the stones brought no sentry's call, Soulai's suspicions deepened.

The two great wooden doors at the main gate rotted on their posts. The one on the left, in fact, had partially pulled away and was hanging at such a precarious angle that Soulai was careful not to touch it as he peeked through the gap. "The whole city's empty," he said in amazement. "There's no one here."

"Except the ghosts of the dead," Habasle responded. Soulai turned. "What?"

"Three kings and eighty years have passed since Sargon the Second built here. He died in battle before sleeping in his own palace—a bad omen. Thus, it's been abandoned." Habasle slid off Ti, obviously in great pain, for he held his side and sagged against the stallion. "I discovered it last year. And if you fancy your limbs, I'd move away from that left door."

Soulai sprang aside. Flushing, he searched his owner's queer smile for a prank. Habasle snickered in an unnerving manner. "Naramsin, my servant at that time, uses his remaining arm to stir a pot in the kitchens. Try your luck at the other door."

By then Soulai would have settled for sleeping beneath the blackening winds, but he knew better than to ignore Habasle's command. Holding his breath, he crept toward the right door and cautiously tested his shoulder against it. A menacing creak rasped the air and he closed his eyes and waited, but nothing fell. He pushed again, and gradually, amid more nerve-wracking creaks and scrapes, the door opened. Habasle shoved his way inside. Soulai coaxed Ti through the narrow entry and was almost trampled when the horse's hip got caught against the door and another loud creak shot him forward in a frightened leap. Somehow the door stayed in place.

"I want Annakum in here, too."

Reluctantly Soulai ducked back outside and scanned the dusky flatland. There was no sign of the mastiff. A section of grasses shivered with the passage of the wind. Or possibly a jackal. Or . . . Soulai shook away images of the uridimmu. He slipped through the entry again.

Habasle was settling himself inside the gatehouse, a narrow, high-roofed building with two small rooms and stairs that climbed to a row of lookout windows. Glazed tiles in red and white and black formed a decorative band around the first room.

"I don't see Annakum," Soulai began hesitantly. "But I think something's wrong with him. I think he's . . . gone mad or something."

"He's not gone mad," Habasle snapped. "He's no doubt decided to keep guard outside the walls tonight. Close the gate, then, and keep Ti close." The braided hobbles hit Soulai in the back as Soulai headed out of the gatehouse. "And don't bother with a fire; I'm burning already."

Soulai carefully shoved the gate to the city closed again and walked to where Ti was hungrily tearing at the dead grasses poking from a dirty trough. His back was hunched against the wind, his tail tucked between his legs. Sand had crusted the lashes around his eyes. Sheltering the stallion's face as best he could, he guided him to a protected corner beside the gatehouse. As he bent to knot the hobbles around Ti's ankles, he wondered why they were needed here within the city's walls. Unless the walls had holes. It had been eighty years. Suddenly he wished for a fire, a big, crackling one. Wild animals wouldn't approach a fire, would they? Not even mad dogs or lions.

When he had removed the rug and bridle and rubbed the sweaty spots smooth, Soulai searched through the darkness for suitable forage. His heart thumped with every step. In a crack beside a wall he found a scrawny sapling and wrenched it from its hold. He carried it back to Ti, who eagerly began ripping the small leaves from the branches. It wasn't nearly enough for the exhausted horse, and Soulai frowned with worry as he patted Ti on the neck and left him for the night.

A dusty haze hid all but the brightest stars now, and a queer burnt smell filled the air. Jackals set up a howling chorus right outside the walls, making Soulai hurry into the gatehouse.

Habasle was already asleep in the center of the first room, one arm bent under his head, the other wrapped around a pouch held close to his stomach. The way he'd drawn up his knees reminded Soulai of how his younger sisters slept.

At least there'd be some peace, he thought, as he made his way to the near corner and sank to the floor. Never in his life had he been so tired. The musty green flavor of the river water rose to his throat and he fought back the urge to vomit again. Wearily he unfastened his sandals and poked at the liquid-filled blisters on his soles. While the air had cooled, a warmth still radiated from the clay tiles, and it soothed his aching legs.

He was sitting there in the dark when a hideous camel spider as big as his hand darted past his feet. The hairy creature raced across the floor and right up and over Habasle's arm to seize a scorpion that had been investigating the pouch. It disappeared just as quickly with its prey.

Soulai's empty stomach growled. Everyone was eating but him, and he began to wonder if there were more figs in Habasle's pouch. He risked the loss of a hand if he was caught. Of course, he might be at risk just looking at the pouch. With his master in such a fevered state, who knew what could happen? He hugged his knees and stared at Habasle. He looked so helpless right now. An unexpected feeling of power grew inside Soulai, such that another rumble from his stomach moved him to action.

As silently as the moonlight drifting across the gatehouse steps, he rose, paused, then tiptoed around Habasle. Holding his breath, he knelt. Slowly he reached out. His stomach gurgled in anticipation. Habasle's breathing changed and Soulai froze. At last he pinched the lip of the pouch and, exhaling, slid it free.

Habasle's eyes shot open. "No! No! No!" he yelled.

His flailing arms knocked the pouch to the floor. "Damn you to Nergal, no!"

Soulai scrambled backward.

A dagger cut the air, jabbing blindly. "I've been waiting, you son of a jackal. You'll never have Ti. Get away!" The black eyes glared but didn't focus, though the knife kept slashing the air. "Fish-headed monster!" Habasle growled. "Red-robed demon!"

The ashipu! Soulai realized, trembling all over. Habasle thought that he was the ashipu, come to kill him.

"It's just me," he blurted in defense, "Soulai. It's me, Soulai."

Habasle blinked. The knife hand fell limp. He shook his head and stared dumbly around the room. Suddenly his eyes closed and he collapsed. Only the rapid rising and falling of his shoulders showed that he was alive. He shivered. "By Ishtar, I'm cold," he mumbled. "Build me a fire."

Still trembling, Soulai ran from the gatehouse and found the branches from the tree that Ti had stripped of leaves. He returned, snapped the twigs into pieces, and piled them in front of Habasle. He waited, then carefully reached for the larger pouch, the one he knew contained a flint. Habasle just lay there, glassy-eyed and moaning slightly.

Between Soulai's cupped hands, the spark caught and

quickly ignited the kindling. He remembered another dead tree, a larger one, and ventured into the night to break off its lower branches and add them to the fire. Soon the light from the blaze was flickering up the four walls of the room. It illuminated bas-relief carvings that showed two men joined in a series of battles against monstrous creatures.

"I thought you were the ashipu." Habasle's voice came low and solemn, almost an apology.

"I know," was all Soulai could bring himself to say.

"He's trying to kill me."

I know that, too, Soulai thought. But out loud he said, "Why don't you tell your father? He's a king; can't he do something?"

Muffled laughter came from the other side of the fire. It stopped and started, climbed and fell, like the senseless chatter of a nervous monkey until Soulai demanded, "What?"

Habasle pointed out the arched doorway at the clearing sky. "See those stars? *They* tell my father who he may see and when. And if he isn't sure, the ashipu tells him." Habasle stopped laughing. In an entirely different voice he said, "In my whole life, I've seen my father only once."

He rested his head on his arm, stared at the fire, and remained quiet. After a while his eyes closed. As time passed, his moaning grew louder, and Soulai could tell that the fever had taken hold again. Habasle mumbled nonsensical words. "Into the darkness," Soulai heard. "All day . . . darkness, white robe . . . figs, no meat . . . emmer, no meat . . ." The words fragmented until Habasle was only tossing his head back and forth and moving his lips in whispers.

Soulai felt a twinge of pity. Habasle's words were tortured by a sickness, to be sure, but at their core was a loneliness much like his own. He, too, had been abandoned by his father. Memories flooded over him: days spent gathering pistachios with his mother, laughing with his younger sisters, secretly sharing his latest clay sculpture with Soulassa. Tears blurred his eyes and he dug his chin into his knees.

In his mind he also saw the lion and the dead goats. And the burned remains of the hut. *Better that you'd never been born*, came the words.

But I'm stronger now, he argued with himself. In two months I've barely touched any clay. I have scars! The disapproving face of his father appeared in Soulai's mind. He wasn't a man yet, it seemed to say. Not yet.

Soulai stared through the doorway at the black sky. A gust of wind sprayed sand against his cheek. His stomach still hurt, but from a different sort of emptiness. Eventually he resigned himself to a miserable night and stretched out on the floor. Just as sleep began to pull over him, Habasle spoke again, this time clearly.

"Damn this worm! It's eating right through me. My other pouch." He held up his hand, and Soulai, fumbling to waken, got up to hand the pouch the short distance. Habasle reached in and pulled out a small clay tablet, much like the ones Soulai had seen in the royal library. He rolled onto his back then, with a pained grunting, and laid it atop his chest. Soulai returned to his corner and silently watched Habasle's strange doings.

"He may control King Ashurbanipal, but he won't hold the reins of King Habasle," he muttered. "The great gods who dwell in heaven and on earth have granted me their favor. Like real fathers, they have raised me. I hear their murmurings in my ear. I read their signs in the sky. I have Ninurta's blessing in Ti and I have this tablet. And now only I will say when the moon disappears." Habasle chuckled. "I'll show him." He chuckled again. "I'll show everyone."

Soulai could make no sense of his owner's boastful words. It was the fever talking, he decided, so he stretched out again and closed his eyes. But he was still awake when the command came.

"Tell me a story."

The words surprised Soulai. When a snicker followed,

however, he doubted their urgency. He waited, listening for the steady breathing that would show that Habasle slept.

"Wake up! Wake up, you good-for-nothing wretch." A palm was slapping the tile floor. Soulai bolted upright. His pity vanished when he saw Habasle's arrogant grin. "I want a story. Now."

With his anger mounting, Soulai sorted through the tales he knew. He tried to reach back to his mountain home, to the times when the storyteller in his uncle's village—

"Just choose one!" Habasle ordered.

"It's from my village," Soulai blurted, scrambling to piece together the story he'd been hearing on the night of the fire. It was an oft-told favorite about a certain lazy fool who spoke vainly and acted stupidly. A malicious sense of mischief overtook him. The story would be perfect. He shivered with the danger of telling it, but, as Habasle was feverish, would he even understand? He cleared his throat and began.

"In a mountain village near ours lived a man who never lifted his hand to any sort of work. He had no family to feed him, and yet he didn't starve. This was because he had convinced the others in his village that he was going to be wealthy some day and that if they would only feed him now, he would feed them all in the future. So, although they had their doubts, the people came to this man every day and gave him some bread, some eggs, and a cup of oil. And every day—"

"No meat?" Habasle interrupted.

"No meat," Soulai replied. "But every day this man—"

"Seems they could have given him a little meat now and then," Habasle argued.

"They didn't give him any meat."

"Not even a thimbleful of ox tongue?"

"No ox tongue, no meat. They gave him bread, eggs, and oil. Do you want to hear the story?"

Habasle mumbled something that ended in a giggle. Soulai pressed his lips together and looked up at the ceiling. He waited for Habasle to be silent before continuing.

"But this man was so lazy that he never cooked anything," he went on, "and so he didn't use the oil. Every day he just dumped the cup of oil which he had been given into a clay jar. And as the jar filled, this man had an idea. 'I'll sell my oil and buy a cow,' he said."

"Then he'd have some meat," came the voice from the other side of the fire. It ended in a loud guffaw.

Infectious laughter started to rise in Soulai's own

throat. He choked it down. When Habasle's chortling turned into moaning, he felt a vengeful satisfaction. Habasle rolled onto his side, clutching his bandaged wound and drawing up his knees. "Continue," he said between short breaths. "Go on, it's a fine story. Truly."

Soulai waited for complete silence before he spoke. This new sense of power thrilled him. "But this foolish man was full of foolish dreams," he said quietly. A little tingle ran up his arms and nape. "And he made great plans. 'The cow will give me calves and they'll grow into cows that will give me more calves and—'"

"And then he'll become a butcher," Habasle interjected with a smirk, but Soulai didn't stop.

"'—and then I'll have a herd of cattle larger than anyone. And I won't live in this little village on the side of a mountain any longer, I'll move to a big house in a big city and I'll have hundreds of servants to tend to my every whim. Then all of the wealthy merchants in this city will parade their most beautiful daughters before me and beg me to make one my bride. And when I have chosen the loveliest of them all, I'll host a huge wedding feast. I'll serve oxen—'"

"Aha!"

Soulai glared.

"'—and camel and mutton and duck. I'll serve beer

and olives and cakes and honey. I'll have music and dancers. And I'll even let the poor fools from the village come sit on the walls to watch me get married.'"

Soulai paused.

"That's it?"

"'And the people in my new city will so admire me that they'll make me their king. Upon my head they'll place a tall crown.' This vain man then picked up the clay jar of oil and balanced it on his head. 'And when they cheer me, I shall graciously bow to the right and to the left'— And with that the clay jar slipped from the man's head, broke into pieces upon the floor, and the oil was lost."

There was a long, dead silence. Soulai fidgeted. Habasle's eyes remained closed, but it wasn't clear if he slept. Deciding at last that he did, Soulai laid down.

"You have told me this story for a reason."

Soulai's sense of power instantly evaporated.

"You believe my plans are as foolish as those of that lazy man, don't you? You rate me an idiot, no saner than he, when, in fact, I am born of the gods." Even though Soulai's eyes were closed, he knew that it was Habasle who now watched *him*; his cheeks burned. "If you value your life at this moment, you'll pray to me for forgiveness."

Soulai clenched his jaw, wavering whether to give up his feigned sleep.

"Pray to me!" the voice roared.

Resentfully, he began the litany. "Lord of my life—"

"Louder!" Habasle demanded.

"—judge of days past and present, forgive me. May your generous heart take pity. Grant me life, though it be worthless, that I may live to serve thee."

"Now," Habasle said smugly, "tell me another story. And save your messages for the thick-headed."

Soulai opened his eyes and glared. "An ant once met a goat by a river," he began. After the harrowing day, his mind was growing cloudy and he struggled to form the story. But before it was finished, Habasle's snoring indicated that he was asleep. "So they cut off the crocodile's tail and they ate the goat," he finished.

He waited. No response this time. Staring out the doorway at the half moon he wondered anew how much of what Habasle said was true. Was he truly born of the gods, as kings were? Could he make the moon disappear? What about the ashipu's plans to murder him and Ti?

And what about the curse—where was the terrible uridimmu now?

ANNAKUM'S HONOR

4

"The worm, it crawled out." Fingers poked Soulai's ribs until Soulai lifted himself onto one elbow and rubbed his eyes. "Look," Habasle said. He raised his tunic to his chest, free of bandages, and pointed to a wound that resembled thin lips parting to reveal a black mouth. An ooze glistened from the swollen opening. But he rocked back on his heels and made a show of thumping his chest with his fist. "I feel strong. The worm took the fever and left me with a lion's hunger, so we're riding back to the river to hunt. I'm not as frugal as the man in your story," he added, grinning. "I need meat."

Soulai didn't miss the pained wince that crossed Habasle's face as he rose, though, and he wondered how well he really felt.

Almost in answer to his question, Habasle suddenly groaned and slapped his forehead. "Damn! My spear." The image of the weapon sailing out over Nineveh on the night of their escape shot through Soulai's mind. But Habasle was already turning a dagger over and over in his hands. "We'll manage something when we get to the river," he said resolutely. He picked up the bridle and tossed it at Soulai. "You go find Ti."

Two nights spent in the cold with little sleep and less food had left Soulai feeling bruised and weakened, and he had to push his body away from the floor. His stomach rumbled loudly.

Although the sky outside the gatehouse was changing from ebony to deep violet, the stars outlining the constellation of the true shepherd still shone overhead. Soulai remembered what Habasle had said about the three stars on the shepherd's belt twinkling, telling that the wings of Ninurta would brush the shoulders of the next king. He gazed at them for a long while, but to his eyes they remained mute.

From nowhere an owl winged directly over his head and just as quickly melted into the predawn gloom. That reminded Soulai that he wasn't the only creature awake in the city, and he hurried on through the vacant marketplace.

In no more than a few steps, a horse's worried nicker reached his ears; his heartbeat quickened. Frantically searching right and left, he strained to pull Ti's silhouette from the darkness. He knew something was wrong.

Finally, as he came around the city's temple, he found him, confined by the hobbles, staring fearfully into the distance. A pair of luminous green eyes at once startled Soulai and mesmerized him, and he froze in place until the shadowy form slipped away noiselessly. He shuddered. His hands were shaking as he reached out to calm Ti. To his dismay, the stallion was quivering as well. They were the same now, he had to admit, cowards both. "I know," he murmured sadly as he stroked the nervous horse. "I know."

The eastern sky had lightened to lavender by the time Soulai and Ti returned to the gatehouse. Habasle had his two pouches packed and slung across his shoulders, and he waited, scowling, while Soulai fastened the rug across Ti's back. Between the two of them, they managed to push the one door wide enough to enable them to squeeze through. Its groaning hadn't ceased echoing when, as Soulai led Ti out, the door fell from its post with a horrific crash.

But Habasle seemed deaf to the noise. "Look," he whispered in awe. He was pointing past the dust-clouded door frame to a faint star hovering low over Dur Sharrukin's eastern skyline. "It's the wandering star of the crown prince, and it's showing itself to *me*." He grinned excitedly and turned to Soulai. "Don't you understand? It's my time."

Annakum came lurching along the wall just then, more gaunt and disheveled than the day before. His pink tongue fluttered halfway to the ground.

"Annakum!" Habasle called. "Ready to *hunt*!" The mastiff trotted past. "Annakum, here!" The command roared through the still morning but died unanswered as the dog plunged drunkenly into the tall grasses and disappeared. "A plague on you then!" Habasle shouted.

Grabbing Ti's mane, he swung his leg and managed to pull himself onto the stallion's back, though not without an unguarded cry of pain. He snugged the reins and, to Soulai's surprise, extended his arm. "I have to hurry. You'll ride." Their hands clasped and before Soulai had his calf wrapped around the other side, Ti bounded off.

A fistful of tunic and the questionable strength of his legs were all Soulai had to keep from falling. Ti's powerful haunches tossed him skyward with each stride, but he didn't dare throw his arms around Habasle again.

By the time they reached the dark green jungle flanking the river, Ti had slowed to a walk. The trio began pushing their way into the scrub. One after another, pockets of damp air submerged them. Croaking frogs fell silent as they approached, then took up their chorus after they passed. Coot flushed in twos and threes, flapping their wings and whistling alarm before ducking into the undergrowth. As the ground turned soft, Ti's steps became tentative. Soulai's own heart thudded with the fear that they were heading into a sticky trap.

Near the river, dense stands of knife-sharp sedge and yellow qasab choked their passage. Habasle slipped from Ti to chop down one of the giant reeds, then fashioned a spear by lashing his dagger to it. They proceeded with the makeshift weapon carried upright and ready.

Greenish black mud sucked at Ti's hooves now. Each careful step started with a soupy squish and finished with a loud pop. A few more slogging steps and Ti sank to his fetlocks, then his knees. He panicked. Habasle and Soulai struggled to hang on as the stallion lunged and leaped and crashed through the tall reeds. With a splash he made it to the river and halted, breathing hard. The sun had risen. Clouds of red and green and yellow bee-eaters swooped arcs around the intruders, twittering anxiously. Annakum poked his head out a little downriver. He looked frantically thirsty, but ignored the water.

Leaning over, Habasle yanked on a young bulrush, which came up easily, root and all. He swished it through the water, then took a bite out of the pale bulb. He pulled up another and handed it to Soulai. Crunching contentedly, he scanned the river, then guided Ti far enough into the shallows to skirt the thickest growth. They waded downriver toward Annakum. Soulai stiffened. As hungry as he was, he couldn't eat. He couldn't even look down. They were in the water again and he vividly recalled it closing over his face. The shore was in view, though, so trying to close his ears to the sloshing of Ti's legs, Soulai focused his eyes on the security of land and prayed to return to it.

As they waded a winding path through tunnels of towering qasab, several deer flushed from the water's edge. The fine-boned creatures hesitated, heads lifted in unison, before darting into the jungle with Annakum barking and chasing after them.

Their narrow trail, which was only a slight flattening of grasses, hardly suited a horse, but Habasle urged Ti along it. Upstart palms and a web of creeping vines hindered their progress until an angry squeal sounded ahead. Habasle thumped Ti's sides and the horse lunged forward, tearing through the undergrowth.

Within a few strides, Ti stopped and snorted. Soulai peered over Habasle's shoulder to see a huge, bristled boar standing on its trampled nest of rushes. Its eyes glinted as it warily sidestepped Annakum. Soulai held his breath as Habasle lifted the makeshift spear and hurled it at the animal. The weapon wobbled and fell short. The boar bolted into the jungle with Annakum close on its jerking tail.

"Get my spear!" Habasle ordered. Soulai had no trouble sliding off Ti's rump, for the horse was prancing and rearing in a panicked frenzy. He quickly picked it up and handed it to Habasle, then hurried to remount, but found himself stepping into air: Habasle was already galloping away on Ti.

Frightened, Soulai sprinted after them. An anguished squeal split the air ahead, and he knew that this time Habasle's spear had found its mark.

But a great crashing followed. Suddenly the boar, with the spear trailing from its bloody shoulder, charged. Soulai jumped sideways. The boar veered after him, catching the spear's shaft on a tree and knocking it free. In desperation, Soulai dived for the weapon. He grabbed it just as the huge animal landed on him. Its odious drool splattered his face. He screamed as the curving yellow tusks slashed his arm.

Grabbing the dagger end of the spear, he shoved it with all his strength into the boar's belly. A blackness was smothering him; his vision blurred, yet somehow he kept jabbing. The meaty weight collapsed on him and he felt the sticky entrails spilling across his thigh. He didn't have the breath to vomit.

Soulai didn't know how long he lay beneath the dead boar. When the heaviness was rolled off him, he looked up to see Habasle wearing that crazed grin of his. But somehow the crashing sounds returned and there was more grunting and Habasle's grin vanished as he madly tugged at the spear still embedded in the boar's body.

Before he was able to free it, Habasle toppled over Soulai, felled by a second angry boar. Annakum hurtled from the undergrowth to sink his teeth into this boar's leg, and with a furious squeal, the pig whirled to fight its new attacker. Yelping and grunting, the fighting animals shook the leafy canopy as Soulai scrambled out from beneath the fray.

From the protection of a tree trunk, he watched Habasle regain his feet and stagger back to the dead boar. He watched him desperately pull at the spear, once again attracting the attention of the boar, which tore away from Annakum to slash at Habasle's leg. The mastiff redoubled his fury and leaped between the two, catching the tusks in his throat. The strangled yelp shot through Soulai. It was more than he could take. Biting his lip, he ran to Habasle's side and helped him wrangle the makeshift spear free. Habasle spun, leveled it, and, with all his strength, buried the point behind the boar's shoulder. The huge animal stumbled backward, step after weaving step, toppled onto its side, and, finally, lay twitching in its death throes.

Shaken but triumphant, Habasle planted a foot on the dying boar. He shared his smile with Soulai, who, to his own surprise, found himself smiling back. They'd done it. They'd cheated death! Habasle's expression changed dramatically, though, as he looked past Soulai. Following his gaze, Soulai saw to his own horror that Annakum lay stretched on the ground, the wound to his neck bubbling with blood. The dog's ribs shuddered spasmodically; with each breath his weak growl trailed to a whimper.

"No." The word formed silently on Habasle's lips as his face went pale. Dropping to his knees, he reached out trembling fingers to stroke Annakum's bloodied head. But instead of a welcome, he was met with a wild snarl that rumbled up through the dog's throat. The massive jaws snapped, narrowly missing Habasle's fingers, and fell back to the ground. The chest deflated and remained motionless.

"Nooooo!" Habasle's wail echoed through the dank jungle air. He sat, unmoving, unbelieving it seemed, and stared at Annakum's body. Tears spilled down his face but he didn't wipe them away. After a long while, he lifted one hand, then the other, and, as custom required, slowly dragged his fingernails across his cheeks. The lines puffed pink, and bled. "No! No! No!" he cried over and over, pounding the earth. True to ritual, he pulled his hair and rubbed handfuls of mud into it, tore at his tunic in a mindless frenzy. When his voice grew hoarse, he drew his knees to his chest and rocked on his heels. "Annakum . . . Annakum . . . Annakum," he chanted.

Tears filled Soulai's eyes as well as he stared at the slumped body of the lifeless dog. He was so tired of blood and injury and death. Miserably he studied the fingers of his left hand, vaguely surprised that he could see right to the bone.

How long they sat there, Soulai couldn't tell, but even with the thick foliage shading their heads, the clearing started to grow hot. The sun must be nearing its peak, he thought absently. His mind wandered to other things, like the ashipu, the uridimmu, and Annakum's strange behavior.

"Do you think it was the ashipu's curse?" he murmured after a time.

"What?"

"The ashipu's curse," Soulai repeated. "I think, maybe, that the uridimmu took the form of a mad dog. He became Annakum. That could mean that it's over."

Habasle sniffled and cleared his throat. "Annakum wasn't mad."

"But you saw him," Soulai insisted desperately. "He couldn't walk straight, he was thirsty but he wouldn't drink . . . when you called he ran away—"

"Annakum never ran away!" Habasle cried. "He was the bravest of all my dogs. From the time he was a puppy I suckled him on the teat of a lioness and he drank in her bravery. There was nothing wrong with him."

"But he tried to bite you—"

"Silence!" Habasle ordered in a raspy voice. He knelt over the mastiff and gently folded his legs beneath him. Then he stood. He began piling rushes and palm fronds on top of the dog's body.

Strangely, Soulai felt no resentment at the harsh command. As he watched Habasle, in fact, he wondered if he'd ever feel anything again. Somehow, he realized that Annakum meant as much to Habasle as Ti did to him. So, cradling his injured limb, he rose to help. The sudden pain that surged along his arm made him gasp, but he gathered what foliage he could.

A whistling snort sounded at the edge of the clearing. With a jolt, Soulai remembered that Ti had been part of the contest. He turned to find the sweaty horse uninjured, but trembling all over. His nostrils flared wide, sucking in the odors of mangled flesh and clotting blood. He stamped his foot. The whites of his eyes showed and their terrified expression reminded Soulai of the head charioteer's angry words: *He's ruined.*

"That's the one who ran away," Habasle said scornfully, "not Annakum."

5
A SHARQI

Yellow flames leaped up to lick the meat strips dangling from the green branch spit. Fat bubbled and dripped, causing the fire to flatten, then hiss and spring twice as high. The carcasses of the two boars lay humped where they had fallen. Their flanks had been hacked open to the bone, attracting masses of black flies.

Habasle tended to the spit; Soulai sat at his side. It was Soulai who rocked back and forth now, for his entire arm throbbed with the pain of his gashed hand. He had wrapped it tightly in a rag torn from the hem of his tunic and he'd tried to cradle it close to his stomach, which ached as well—from the huge amount of food he had devoured. But in a bizarre way, Soulai felt better than he had in days.

Ti was hobbled on the edge of the clearing, apart from the smoke. He stood slack-hipped, dozing. Soulai wanted to know what had happened, why Ti had been accused of running away, but Habasle just sat staring into the fire as he had since they'd finished eating. He didn't even turn his head when the smoke drifted into his face. Trying to forget his pain, Soulai focused his hearing on the river birds' cries of coming twilight, on the occasional splash and ensuing ripple against the shore, on the fire's vibrant crackle.

Dusk had started to close in when Habasle lifted his reddened eyes and spoke.

"I've been thinking on it all day . . . and I still don't understand," he said in a cracked voice. "It's *one* death. I've watched countless dogs go down in the hunt. Why am I crying over this one?"

Soulai didn't know how to answer, wasn't sure if he even needed to. Habasle seemed to be talking to himself as much as anyone.

"When Annakum was born," he continued quietly, "the keeper of the hounds told me he was a runt, that he was too weak to live, and he threw him out under the sun. I happened across him later—blind, whimpering—but"—he shrugged—"with this dumb courage he was dragging his body, one step at a time, to—I don't know—someplace, someplace other than an empty death." He heaved a sigh. "I knew that day that he had something to prove and that he had the strength to do it, so I set about giving him more. There was a tame li-

173

oness in the zoo and I suckled him on her teats. And he grew bigger and fatter and stronger than any of his brothers." His shoulders shook as he fought to control the sobs. "But he's just a dog. There's a hundred more back at the kennel. So why am I crying?" His pleading look begged a response from Soulai.

"Because he saved you," Soulai offered tentatively. It didn't matter if the mastiff had been mad or sick or whatever. Soulai had been there; he'd witnessed the animal's bravery. "He gave his life for yours," he added. "So he wouldn't die an empty death." Such talk made him uncomfortable and he cast his eyes to the ground.

He waited for Habasle's scornful laughter, but when there was only silence, he cautiously lifted his eyes. His glance was met by a somber face. "I think you're right," Habasle said. "And I think, maybe, I'll be joining him soon. Maybe we'll hunt together in the underworld."

The weak smile couldn't water down the horror of his words. Soulai's eyes widened. "What are you saying?"

Habasle shrugged again and sighed. He dropped his hands to his lap, then raised them and began counting on his fingers. "The ashipu is trying to kill me." He folded his thumb. "There is a hole in my side that worms use for their comings and goings." He folded his index finger. "An uridimmu may still be tracking me." He looked at Soulai. "I guess it's possible that the uridimmu may have taken Annakum's form, but that doesn't mean it's dead. The amulet still lies in my pouch."

"Then let's throw it in the river," Soulai exclaimed. "Let's be rid of it."

Habasle shook his head. "It will have other uses." He folded his middle finger. "My horse, the gift of the god Ninurta, has failed me." Another finger went down. "And you," he looked directly at Soulai, "I imagine you would not hesitate to lift a knife to my back, would you?" Holding Soulai's stunned gaze, he bent his little finger.

"Now," he stated in a tired yet matter-of-fact manner, "we'll stay with Annakum for three days until his spirit has found its way to the underworld. Elul is almost over, but Tisri is still a good month to begin a battle, so I'll return to Dur Sharrukin and plan my fate. Annakum shall not be alone in his honor."

Habasle set to work on his dagger then, rubbing the blade in slow circles in the gritty earth and periodically wiping it clean on his tunic. He continued the silent, ritual polishing for three days. The few times he stopped were to direct Soulai to wrap the cooked meat in palm leaves and pack as much of it as possible in his two pouches, though he himself refused to eat. When Habasle was tired, he lay with his head on a folded arm, eyes open, staring into the fire. Whether Habasle slept, Soulai couldn't say, for each morning when Soulai awakened, Habasle was already sitting up, polishing his knife.

The three carcasses rotted quickly in the jungle's heat. The stench was noxious at first, but by the third day, when a worm dropped out of Annakum's nose, Soulai hardly noticed it. Habasle stared at the wriggling white creature for a moment; he seemed to be settling something in his mind. Then he stood. "Let's go," he said quietly.

Their trek out of the jungle seemed to go faster than their journey into it, and by midafternoon they were plodding up the grassy rise toward Dur Sharrukin. The sky, which usually shone a brilliant blue, burned deadly white. The heads of the grasses bowed before a hot wind that rushed out of the south. Habasle was hunched atop Ti, and Soulai walked in the lee shelter of Ti's left haunch. Halfway up the hill, a sudden whirlwind stung Soulai with sand and bits of rock, nearly knocking him off his feet. In the next breath the plain fell eerily silent. Soulai glanced up, hoping to see Dur Sharrukin's walls, but another strong gust blinded him. More dust and sand and bits of leaves pelted him until the air itself became something palpable, a swirling gray curtain that closed around them. Soulai feared that they were traveling in circles. The veiled sun blazed orange briefly, then was snuffed from sight. The sky darkened and the dust-filled air glowed a coppery hue. It shifted and swirled about them until Soulai lost sense of land or sky, day or night.

Habasle finally pulled Ti to a halt and slid from his back. "It's no use," he shouted against the whistling gale. "It's a sharqi, a black wind. We'll have to wait it out." He jerked his thumb at Ti, who curved his head around as if listening to the plan. "Make him lie down."

Soulai hesitated, reluctant to make Ti serve as a windbreak, but Habasle had already begun yanking on the bit and shouting at the stallion, who braced his neck in confusion. So Soulai worked his way around, against the wind, bent over, and lifted Ti's right foreleg. As he had learned in the palace stable, he tucked it high, close to the shoulder. Then he reached over the withers and, clumsily tightening the rein with his bandaged hand, began pulling the horse's nose around. Giving in to the pressure, Ti stretched his muzzle closer and closer to his left flank until he became so unbalanced on three legs that he collapsed onto the ground with a grunting thud.

"Get out of my way," Habasle said as he yanked his robe from Ti's back. He wrapped it around his head and shoulders and took shelter beside Ti's belly. "At least he's good for something," he muttered.

As Soulai settled himself beside Ti's neck he glared at Habasle. He coaxed the horse's head around, tucked the reins under his elbow, and caressed the dust-covered forehead apologetically. Ti nickered softly.

After a while, Habasle curled onto his side, his back to Ti. Though blowing sand stung Soulai's neck and ears, he remained upright, cradling the massive head in his lap. The wind's relentless onslaught, its monotonous wail, finally numbed him into a drowsy half-sleep.

It was the silence that awakened him. That and a clamping chill. When Soulai opened his eyes, the first thing he noticed was that Ti no longer rested his head in his lap, but instead stared expectantly into the twilight. Soulai's heart thudded. What was out there? Rubbing the grit from his eyes, he scanned the horizon. To his surprise, Dur Sharrukin's walls loomed no farther than the flight of two arrows. They had been so close.

Ti abruptly lunged to his feet and shook, though his brilliant gold-and-white markings remained covered with dust. Jostled awake, Habasle rolled onto his knees. A film of dirt coated his face as well, and he opened and closed his mouth as if tasting something awful.

"Look," Soulai said, pointing to Dur Sharrukin.

Habasle barely glanced up, then struggled to his feet

and moved around Ti. "The ashipu is gaining power," he mumbled. He slapped at Ti's shoulder, brushing away the dirt that concealed the hawklike marking. "Even over Ninurta!"

"Let's get inside Dur Sharrukin," Soulai said. But Habasle was watching the huge moon, partially concealed by silver-yellow clouds, rise from the horizon.

"When the rising moon is half-hidden by clouds," he recited, "so that only the lower half is visible, Assyria will be invaded by an enemy. And there will be great mourning for a prince." He leaned against Ti, his jaw tense. His hand found its way to his side and he slumped a little. "I don't feel right," he murmured. "I think maybe the worm has returned . . . or the ashipu's curse . . . Annakum's sickness. I feel the drool building in my throat." He opened and closed his mouth several more times.

When he looked at Soulai, the fever once again showed itself in his eyes. And this time a look of desperation accompanied it. "I can't do this alone," he said. "You have to ride for help."

Soulai was stunned. "Me?"

For a moment Habasle seemed to want to take back his words, but then he slowly nodded. "Yes. It's your duty."

But in the black eyes Soulai detected an anxiousness that lay behind the command. This boy who was his master was even more ill than he let on, and he knew in that instant that they both sensed the balance of power tipping.

"There's enough moonlight," Habasle said, mustering his composure. "Take the horse and ride back to Nineveh. I'm commanding you," he reminded Soulai. "Find Naboushoumidin, the royal scribe. He can consult his tablets. There must be some help for me."

Up along Dur Sharrukin's walls, the jackals howled, sending a tickle of fear through Soulai. He suddenly wanted no part of his new role. "I don't know the way," he protested. "And . . . and how can I enter the palace, alone and at night?"

Habasle tugged the hammered silver bracelet from his wrist and extended it to Soulai. With resignation in his voice, he said, "Take it." Then he pulled the robe from his shoulders. "Put this on, too."

Soulai took the items but stood dumbly.

"Others have said we resemble one another." Habasle's words came clipped and matter-of-fact as he removed his personal cylinder seal, which was elegantly carved from blue chalcedony. He tentatively offered it to Soulai, changed his mind, and pulled it back. For a long time he studied the necklace. Finally he heaved a long sigh and extended his arm again. "My identity," he said, looking directly into Soulai's face. "And with it, my life."

Soulai hesitated. Slowly he removed the tag that marked him a slave and exchanged it for the cylinder seal. With his heart pounding in his ears, he placed the new necklace over his head. A vigorous sense of power surged within him and he couldn't contain the grin that spread across his face, though he tried to squelch it when he read the uneasy look on Habasle's.

"Don't crow yet. The ashipu is not my only enemy."

"Do you really think I can get to Naboushoumidin?" The idea of galloping Ti for help so enthralled Soulai that he ignored Habasle's warning. He fitted the silver bracelet onto his right forearm, just as Habasle wore it, then slipped into the warm robe, luxuriously soft and weighty. "I might be able to get inside the city, but the palace guards will look closer."

"Hmm." Habasle frowned. He counted on his fingers. "Tomorrow is the first of the week. In the afternoon Naboushoumidin tells his stories beneath the lamassu of the palace's west gate. There will be a great crowd. Make your way to the front and tell him—and only him—of my condition, and command his help."

Soulai looked down the grassy slope at the black ribbon of trees that hid the river—the river where he'd almost drowned. His excitement vanished. "Why don't we ride back to Nineveh together?" he proposed suddenly. "Ti can carry both of us. Or you can ride and I'll walk."

Habasle shook his head. "I fear I won't be riding for a long time . . . if ever again. The ashipu's power is stronger than I thought, though I do possess something that he badly needs." He patted the smaller pouch.

"What will you do?"

"I'll crawl inside Dur Sharrukin—a little worm myself—and wait. I have my dagger to fight off the vultures . . . or anyone who turns on me." His hollow grin couldn't hide his worry. Soulai started to turn away, but Habasle had one more order. "Whatever happens," he said solemnly, "don't let the ashipu get his hands on this horse."

Soulai shook his head. No one would steal the stallion from him. "Are you sure you don't want to ride Ti at least up to Dur Sharrukin's gates?"

"I'm dying as we speak," Habasle said heavily as he lowered himself to the ground. "Don't argue the details." With an all-out effort he waved his arms in the air. "Go on! Ride!"

Excitement poured through his veins as Soulai turned and gathered the reins on Ti's withers. Unable to use his injured hand to support a leap, he jumped high enough to get himself across the horse's back, then pulled his leg over. The stallion sprang forward, making Soulai gasp and snatch the reins tighter. What if I can't stay on? he worried suddenly. What if he throws me out there in the middle of nowhere? Adjusting the reins and settling his seat seemed to calm Ti. Still, the stallion pranced in place with such awesome power that Soulai was at a loss for words. How could Habasle think this most magnificent of horses had failed him?

"What happened?" Soulai blurted. "With the boar— what happened to Ti?"

Habasle narrowed his eyes. "The boar was coming at us," he said flatly. "I spurred Ti toward him but at the last instant he showed himself faithless and fled. Now go!"

Even before Soulai could loosen the reins, Ti grabbed the bit in his teeth and trotted off down the slope, obviously anxious to get home. As they picked up speed, the trot became a canter and the canter a gallop. Faster and faster, Ti hurtled headlong over the undulating land, and Soulai's tugs on the reins did nothing to slow him. Stiff with fear, Soulai finally managed to brace his knees against the stallion's sides, give one hard yank on the right rein, and pull Ti's head almost around to his flank. Even if we fall, he figured, at least we'll have stopped. I'll be able to catch my breath.

Ti didn't fall, though, and Soulai pulled him into a

blowing, walking circle. When his own legs had stopped trembling, Soulai took a moment to look around. Dur Sharrukin's walls were barely visible beyond the hill behind them. The rolling grasslands stretched in all directions, shored up only by the winding trees and river to the west. A little to the south and east, darkly silhouetted against the moonlit sky, rose the mountains of his village.

A sharp homesickness overcame him, quickly replaced by the anger he still felt toward his father.

Better that you'd never been born ... never been born ... never been born!

The cutting words drummed through his head. His father had bartered him, had sent him away. He'd said Soulai needed scars to be a man. Soulai's hand throbbed harder with the memory. Well, he had his scars. What's more, he sat astride a royal stallion, was dressed in jewels and a fine robe—better than any his father owned. Who was the man now?

Staring at the mountains, Soulai felt his heart beat faster. It would be easy to gallop back to his village, show off Ti to his family, and still make it back to Nineveh before tomorrow afternoon. He eased the stallion in that direction. But after a few steps he reined him to a halt. Habasle might be very sick, he conceded, so sick he might die. What if he dies before I get back? Would his death be my fault?

Tormented by a storm of conflicting passions, Soulai kept circling Ti and thinking. The sky became black, and the grasslands glowed silver under the giant moon. A dusty, burnt scent hung in the air, giving off an odor of things finished and, at the same time, of things not yet begun. It smelled like the day after the fire, when his life had been forced to change.

Soulai tugged on the reins once more. Before the moon had set, he was climbing the mountain path toward his home.

HOMEWARD

Soulai had never herded his goats this far along the mountain range, but he felt safer traveling through the tree-covered slopes than out in the open grasslands. He knew if he climbed at a shallow angle, he was likely to come across the stone aqueduct that carried spring water down to Nineveh.

Ti was unhappy climbing the mountain and his nervous prancing was increasingly harder to control. He kept shaking his head, which jerked the reins out of Soulai's hand; and every little noise from the surrounding woodlands made him snort and come to a halt, twitching with fear.

Soulai laid a soothing hand on the horse's neck. The boar hunt had done this to him, he knew, just as the lion hunt had before that. How could a creature who had once captured all eyes with his nobleness and bravery now be so timid? An unseen animal rustled the grasses just then, making Ti jump a full stride sideways. Soulai bit his lip. Maybe I shouldn't ride Ti back to Nineveh at all, he thought. What future does he have there? Murder at the hands of the ashipu? Death on the battlefield? The brilliant parti-color stallion whose destiny he'd wanted to share seemed to have fallen far short of his promise. They were cowards both.

Ti startled and shied again. Soulai had to prod him forward. The adventure of returning home was losing its excitement; disappointment and a sense of sadness weighed upon him.

In the darkness ahead, he finally made out a pale snakelike form. He kept blinking as he rode closer, wanting to believe he had found the way home, and when the sound of running water reached his ears, he sighed with relief. Taking a firm hold on Ti's mane, he headed him up the path that flanked the aqueduct.

Soulai tipped his head and gazed at the starry sky as Ti climbed. It occurred to him that Habasle might be staring up at the same stars. He'd be wondering, no doubt, how far Soulai had ridden. Guilt stabbed him. He shunted it aside and looked up again. The constellation of the scorpion was gone. There was the long-necked bird, though, winging its way south and west—back toward Nineveh, he noticed. And there was the giant horse now, galloping in its wake. That image made him pause. But the stars had to be wrong. Nineveh was a place for warriors. He clenched his jaw and rode on.

The sky beyond the mountain's crest was just lightening to an iron gray when Soulai came upon the burned-out remains of his family's house. The charred walls stood silent, encompassing only the few brick piles his mother had stacked that first morning some three months ago. He couldn't help scanning the remains for his clay horses, though he distinctly remembered Soulassa gathering them up as he was being led away. The pleasure he had once felt when cradling a lump of clay returned with such a strong pang that it surprised him. But that was when he was a child, he scolded himself, and he tried to set aside the memory. He coaxed Ti onward.

The village was just stirring. A cock crowed atop a slanting roof; an old man peed alongside a hut. Some children carrying pouches to fetch water spotted Soulai and ran toward him with shouts that splintered the quiet.

"It's Soulai! It's Soulai!"

The children swarmed around him, touching the splendid fringed rug and the sleek hide of the stallion. Soulai was about to warn them to be careful, but to his amazement the gold-and-white neck stretched down and Ti stood as still as one of Soulai's statues, allowing the children to pat his forehead.

"Soulai? Soulai, is that you?" Two men, friends of his father, emerged from their homes and made their way toward him.

"Welcome home, boy!" said one, clapping him on the thigh.

"Where's my family?" Soulai asked.

His heart skipped a beat when the men shook their heads. "So sad, so sad," they murmured together. "They live now with your aunt and uncle," the first man said. He pointed in the direction of the neighboring village as if Soulai had been away so long he wouldn't remember.

Worry grew in him as he guided Ti across the streambed. This wasn't how he had pictured his homecoming.

The unfamiliar sound of horse hooves entering the next village brought dozens of heads popping out of doorways. As before, the children were the first to crowd around Ti. Among the adults that followed, Soulai found his uncle, and then his father.

"That's surely a creature of the gods you're riding," his uncle said appreciatively. The man circled Ti, taking in every line of the handsome stallion.

Soulai's father moved toward them. He laid an uncertain hand on his son's leg and appeared to be searching for words. Noticing the bandaged hand, he said, "You're hurt."

Tears threatened to rush to Soulai's eyes. Of course I'm hurt, he wanted to cry. You did this to me. But he stuck out his chin instead. "Just a scar," he responded.

The words hit their mark. His father blanched.

"You've been set free?"

"I was given this horse to ride."

"Jahdunlim . . . ?"

"Jahdunlim sold me to the palace," he said angrily.

Soulassa came pushing her way through the onlookers and when Soulai saw her, he smiled.

"You're home!" she exclaimed. "And your horse! He looks just like—" She raised her hand. "Wait here." Sprinting back to their aunt and uncle's hut, she disappeared inside, then rushed out again, carrying something. She handed Soulai one of his clay figurines, the one of the long-maned stallion standing with his head thrust boldly into the wind. "It looks exactly like him," she said in amazement. "How did you know?"

Soulai studied the statue. It did look like Ti, he thought in surprise. Or what Ti used to look like. And the clay, even hardened, felt good.

"I've kept them all," Soulassa was saying, "including the broken ones. They're in a safe place, waiting for you."

"Thank you." He hesitated, disliking the awkward-ness of his return. "I thought you'd be a wife by now."

Soulassa glanced at her father.

"That's not in the stars," he said gruffly. "Soulai, go to your mother now. Maybe the sight of you will make her well. Your sister will see to the horse."

Soulai slid off Ti and handed the reins to Soulassa. The lingering blisters on his feet stung the moment he touched ground, and he ripped off the palace-issued san-dals and tossed them into the undergrowth. He curled his toes in the powder-soft dirt.

Ducking inside the hut, Soulai found his mother sit-ting slack-legged on a mat. Between her hands, his baby brother practiced sitting upright. His aunt, who had been carding some leftover wool beside the cooking pot, dropped the brush to the floor with a clatter.

His two younger sisters jumped up from their play and ran to him, hugging his leg. "Soulai! Soulai! Soulai!" they squealed in unison. When his heavy robe parted to reveal the scars on his thigh, their eyes widened.

Soulai tousled the girls' thick hair. "Don't you worry," he said, smiling. "The lion looks worse." His smile faded, though, as he studied his mother. Like a child, he fell into the cradle of her arm. Burying his face against her neck, he inhaled the familiarity of home. His mother squeezed him close, her shoulders trembling. The trembling became sobs which led to coughing—such heavy coughing that she had to push Soulai away.

Quietly entering the hut, Soulassa took a place beside their mother. Her hands remained folded in her lap, her head bowed, and Soulai realized it was the first time that he had seen his sister look helpless.

As the coughing worsened, the baby started crying at being jostled. Soulai's mother turned her head, coughed harder, and spit. She lifted her tunic then, pushed her nipple into the wailing mouth, and smiled wanly at Soulai.

"Look at you," she said, fingering the edge of his beautiful robe. "How handsome."

"No," said Soulai, gently taking her hand in his. "Tell me about you. Are you sick? Why are you living here?"

Soulai's aunt had returned to her wool, but now she stopped. "Of course she's sick—her heart's broken. Her eldest son a slave, her daughter rejected."

"You aren't getting married?" Soulai asked, turning to Soulassa.

His sister shook her head.

"After the fire we couldn't put enough together for the dowry," his mother explained. "The little we had went to purchase new tools so your father could work."

"And speaking of work, what are you doing here?" his aunt demanded. "Has the debt been repaid?"

Soulai sat back on his heels, aware that villagers had gathered outside the doorway, awaiting his story. He described Nineveh's palace and the stables filled with beautiful horses. Hiding a growing sense of guilt, he told of his service to the prince, Habasle, which brought appreciative aahs from the crowd. He embellished a few tales of hunting lions and boars and finished by saying that he and Habasle were out together on a many-days hunt and that he had been given permission to ride home.

A voice came from the doorway: "So you have repaid your debt?"

Soulai's back stiffened. "I'm home, aren't I?"

"But the term was five years. How has the debt been repaid?"

"The debt is my father's, not mine."

"Soulai!" Disappointment sounded in his mother's voice.

Bolting for the door, he pushed through the crowd, and found his way to Ti. He fumed, mad at all of them and, he had to admit, at himself. Soulassa was quickly at his side, stroking Ti's neck.

"Don't worry about me, Soulai," she said. He could

tell she was trying to sound brave. "I can marry some-one else . . . some other time."

"Here." Soulai slid Habasle's silver bracelet off his arm and handed it to his sister. "This alone should make up your dowry."

She gazed with wonder at the extravagant piece of jewelry before handing it back. "I'm guessing this isn't yours to give." She studied his face for a long time, then said, "You've spun a tale for the others, Soulai, but you've never lied to me. So please tell me the truth. Why do you wear these clothes?" Her hand flicked disdainfully at Habasle's robe. "And why do you ride this fancy horse? And how has the debt of our family been repaid?"

With a deep sigh, Soulai told her everything.

His sister's eyes widened as he spoke. "You're killing an innocent man," she whispered in horror.

"I haven't killed anyone!" he protested.

"But you've left this prince wounded . . . and sick . . . in an empty city. You've stolen his horse, Soulai."

"But I haven't—" he tried to interrupt. A wave of his sister's hand closed his mouth.

"If, as you say, you are the only person who knows where he is, then you *are* killing him as we speak."

A small cry escaped Soulai. "I just wanted to see you," he said. "I wanted you to see that I'm a man now."

"In whose eyes?" Soulassa demanded. *"His?"* He knew she meant their father. "Or in yours? You're nothing like him," she went on impatiently, "so why do you keep measuring yourself by his stick? You can't stay here; you have to go back; that's where your destiny lies."

"You mean my death, don't you?" he retorted. "I've already been mauled twice, and near to drowned once. I won't last the five years, Soulassa." His throat constricted. "I'm too much a coward for that life," he said quietly.

To his surprise, Soulassa lifted his bandaged hand. "The way I look at it," she said, "you're rather brave: You've escaped the lion, survived the river, and triumphed over the boar. There's still plenty of living in you. And creating, I think."

She was searching his eyes for agreement, but Soulai looked away. "There's no creating back there," he said belligerently. "It's all killing and dying; it's time passed in the underworld." She said nothing, which annoyed him. "You don't understand," he concluded. "You don't care."

"One of the things you've said is true"—Soulassa finally responded with an edge to her voice—"I don't understand you right now. But I do care. We all do."

He was casting around. "Father doesn't. He traded me off like an animal."

Soulassa's eyes narrowed. "Somebody had to pay, Soulai. It wasn't fair, perhaps, and it wasn't easy—even for him. He's carried the guilt all summer. And Mother cries nonstop whenever someone mentions your name." She paused. "But he did what he had to do. He did what he thought was right for the family."

"You think it's right? Wait until you marry and have children; then you come tell me it's right to sell your child!"

However soft her voice, Soulassa's look was still full of reproach. "But you're not a child, Soulai."

The words slapped him across the face. He clenched his fists. "I'm not going back—not yet!"

"Of course you're not." Their father had joined them. He spoke in a commanding voice, threw his arm around his son's shoulders, and hugged him in a way that Soulai could not remember ever having experienced before. "You're home. And it's seeming that there are two men in the family now."

RACING THE SUN GOD

7

Before long, Soulai was sitting cross-legged on the floor of his uncle's crowded hut. The villagers had left the doorway to go about their morning chores, yet an air of expectancy hung about the house, and Soulai could sense their cocked ears and readiness to return in a rush.

A bowl was set in his hands by his aunt. He felt her glare lingering on him as she straightened. He'd never been a favorite with her—his love of clay had brought the word *worthless* to her lips—and now his suspected lies only fed her disapproval. "Thank you," he murmured before spooning the honeyed milk curds into his mouth. Soulassa had added a handful of chopped almonds on top, the way he liked, yet he found no flavor in them this morning, and the milk turned instantly sour in his stomach. The pain made him think of

Habasle and his worm. Was he still alive? His stomach again twisted with guilt and he set down his bowl.

"Are you all right?" his mother asked. She hadn't taken her teary eyes off of him.

"Of course he's all right," his father answered in his stead. "Didn't I tell you your son would return a man? Just take a look. Now he's got some—"

Every head in the room lifted.

"—got something to be proud of," his father substituted, and Soulai flinched, knowing he meant *scars*. "He's as much a man as me."

Soulai glanced at Soulassa, who raised an eyebrow before turning away. She and their aunt had settled themselves apart from the others. He knew they whispered about him. Discomfort needled him from all sides.

"Tell us about that horse you have with you," his uncle said.

"His name is Ti," Soulai began. How foreign the subject seemed here. When had his family ever discussed horses? "He comes from the horsebreeders of Lake Urmia."

"And what has he been bred to do?"

Soulai hesitated. "He's been bred to carry a soldier to war, or to pull a chariot. Or to ride into the hunt. Did you see his odd-colored eyes? The head charioteer said that horses like him aren't even afraid of lions." His voice faltered.

"And just when do you suppose we'll have our next war, Soulassa?" His aunt's cutting remark was clearly meant for him. He didn't hear his sister's response.

"Wife!" his uncle warned. But he turned to Soulai with a look of concern upon his face.

"What plans *do* you have for this horse? He looks as though he's used to a ration of grain and we've none of that here."

"He'll keep on grass," Soulai answered none too confidently.

"Of course he will," his father added. "At least until Jahdunlim climbs the mountain again. I know he'll pay a fistful of silver for the likes of him."

Soulai looked at his father with shock.

"I'm not selling Ti."

"Oh, come now. What are we going to do with a royal warhorse up here?"

Soulai stood. "Ti stays with me," he said, and he turned and ran out of the hut once again.

Before he was three steps outside, Soulassa was at his elbow. She tried to lay a hand on his arm, but he shook it off.

"Where are you going, Soulai?"

"What do you care?"

A strangled sound came from her throat and she stamped her foot. "You know I care—but do *you*? Do you care about this horse who's been bred to face lions? About that prince who's asked you to save his life?" Her voice trembled with anger. "And what about the rest of us? You can wear these clothes and ride this horse for a while, but . . ." She threw up her hands. "How long before they come looking for you?" Soulai knew everybody around slowed to listen. "And if they can't find you, what will Nineveh's soldiers do to us?"

People were gathering around them now, not hiding their interest. Soulai felt like a snake was wrapping its coils around him, slowly choking him. "If you make me go back, I'll be a slave again," he said desperately. "Is that what you want?"

Soulassa glanced skyward, sucked in her breath, then looked straight at him. "I'm not *making* you go back. I can't. But"—she hugged herself and blinked back tears—"but for years you told me that you didn't fit in here, that you felt useless. Don't prove yourself right. Or him," she whispered.

For a moment Soulai wasn't sure what she meant, but then, from the surrounding crowd, he could sense his father's smirk.

"You have to choose," Soulassa said. "Now."

It was the same demand Jahdunlim had made. And Habasle.

For the first time since he'd made the decision to ride home, Soulai faced the nagging uneasiness he'd tried to keep buried in the pit of his stomach. He turned his back on his sister and the others and gave Ti a good, hard look. Still coated with dust and streaked with sweat, the stallion foraged through some fallen leaves like any one of the village's donkeys. That would be his future here. Soulassa was right; there was nothing here for either of them.

Trying to keep his hands from shaking, Soulai set about refastening the rug on Ti, along with the breast-collar and crupper. It was the first act of bravery in his life and, truth be told, he was scared. He tossed the reins over the stallion's neck and, taking a deep breath, mounted. With a last look at his sister, one punctuated by an attempt at a confident smile, Soulai urged Ti forward.

A glimpse of something pale caught his eye just before a loud crack announced that Ti's hoof had crushed it. Soulai pulled Ti to a stop. On the ground lay the broken remains of his clay horse, the pride of his childhood. He paused for a moment, staring at it, then thumped his heels. Ti bounded down the path. As they plummeted, the cold morning air rushed against Soulai's face like a watery current. His breath came in short gasps, but each one cleansed him and felt good.

His mind raced ahead of their descent. It had taken two days walking to reach Nineveh with Jahdunlim. Could Ti gallop that distance in less than half the time? Already he could feel the first rays of the sun god Shamash warming his back. Naboushoumidin would be telling his stories this very afternoon. A worry grew in him that he'd started too late. He should never have ridden home. Now there wasn't enough time.

Still, when the ground leveled at the base of the foothills, he bent over Ti's neck and urged him on. The stallion doubled his speed. With every muscle, Soulai concentrated on keeping his balance, for he was fully aware of the bone-shattering earth below. Sweat soon beaded his brow, and Shamash laughed at him from above, but Soulai gritted his teeth and rode on. He'd show them, he swore. He'd show all of them.

PART 3

Pink-orange light streamed through the crate's slats, painting a pattern across velvety paws. The lion studied the stripes with a bored expression that masked his longing. He shifted his haunches. The rough wood needled his hip. He shifted again. But his underleg relaxed into his own excrement and he tucked it up. The muscle cramped. Amid the uneasy chitter of other awakening animals, he groaned.

Man had done this. Man had snatched him from freedom. In sudden fury, the lion snarled and spun; he swiped at the thick planks, shoved his massive head against the door. It gave, just a little. Curious, he pawed at the door's edge. It wiggled.

Steadying his golden eyes on the spot, he began pushing. He caught only splinters at first, but kept at it. The pawing grew frantic, and little by little the door relented. The lion thrust a foreleg through. He leaned into it. *The wood squealed, then slowly gave way in splintering pops.*

Shredded slats combed through his mane as he squeezed through the opening. For the first time in a long time he stood at his full height. The tuft on his long tail swatted the broken crate in parting contempt.

Voices were approaching. The lion crouched, scanned the zoo for cover, and in three graceful leaps bounded atop the contents of a storage shed. He crouched in the shadows of the thatched roof. He was hungry. Man was here. It was time to feed.

THE TRAP 1 UNSEEN

As the morning wore on, Ti's sides began to glisten. Then the sweat turned to sticky lather that glued Soulai's legs to the horse's coat. Although they alternated between trotting and galloping, the stallion's breathing gave way to labored gusts. His neck, usually arched, hung level, straining to pull his body along. Soulai knew they should rest; what if Ti went lame? But the possibility of Habasle's death weighed on him. I won't fail at this, he said with determination. He pressed his heels harder into Ti's flanks and the stallion, sensing the urgency, responded.

When they reached the main road leading to Nineveh, Soulai eased his kicking and allowed Ti to walk. With caravans of herdsmen and merchants crowding the road, progress was slow anyway. Soulai thought about trotting around the knots of people and animals, but fretted about attracting attention. What if someone questioned his identity? He glanced up at the sky. The sun god was already sailing past his summit.

To his dismay, heads began to turn. Ti, even lathered and blowing, was still a magnificent animal. And Soulai, dressed as a noble, was obviously in a great hurry. Something important was afoot. Herdsmen whispered. A mother roused her children from a heavily laden oxcart and pointed. The unfamiliar attention made Soulai throw back his shoulders with pride. Then, remembering his sister's words about wearing clothes of deceit, he squirmed beneath the scrutiny.

Ahead, a flock of lop-eared sheep blocked the roadway, and past them, Nineveh loomed into sight. The scent of home made Ti restless and he began to prance. Tossing his head, he pulled the reins from Soulai's hands. Soulai quickly gathered them back; he spoke sharply, but Ti reared and spun. The sheep scattered, bleating in alarm, and their herdsmen, having noticed Soulai's regal attire, bowed slavishly and urged him to take the road. He had no choice but to loose the reins.

Head held high, Ti trotted on until the crowded road was once again obstructed, this time by a long caravan of plodding oxen. Some pulled wagons loaded high with bundled goods, while others lumbered alongside, free of harness. The owner of this wealth was a man on horseback who, distracted by the noisy cries of the frightened sheep, had turned to look over his shoulder. When he spotted Ti, his gaze changed to one of lingering appreciation. Soulai's stomach dropped. Jahdunlim!

What am I going to do? he screamed inwardly. Jahdunlim would certainly recognize him if he got a close look. Pretending to check the crupper securing the rug, he pulled Ti to a halt and turned his back to the road. He fiddled with it as long as he could, but the stallion began tossing his head and bucking with impatience.

"That is a fine-looking horse you ride."

Soulai jumped. It was Jahdunlim's oily voice; he'd know it anywhere. Ti whinnied a challenge to the man's gelding.

"He wouldn't be for sale, would he? I've just returned from trading in Harran and I've silver to offer." Jahdunlim jingled the pouch he wore on his belt.

Soulai shook his head, trying to hide his face. He kept busying himself with the crupper, but the man didn't go away.

"There is always another horse, isn't there? And there is always so much you can do with silver," he said in that slithery way of his. "Why, you could buy yourself a slave—or another slave, as a person of your position no doubt already owns a great number of them." The trader reined his gelding around Ti, peering suspiciously at Soulai. "But slaves can be so much trouble," he rambled on, "wouldn't you agree? So maddening when they run off. Which is why much of my trade is in slaves who forget they are slaves. I firmly believe that when a possession is found away from its owner, it is only right for the finder to see that the possession is returned to its rightful place. For an appreciative fee, of course."

By now he had worked his way directly under Soulai's face. It only took one look for an "Aha!" to jump from his lips. Greedily, he grabbed Ti's reins. Soulai panicked. On impulse, he kicked Ti toward the gelding, forcing the smaller horse to shy away. Jahdunlim ended up teetering between the two horses, reluctant to release the reins, but at the last moment he spat a curse and let go. Soulai yanked Ti toward Nineveh, urging him into another gallop. He didn't care who noticed him now.

In and out and around the startled travelers they raced, until they reached a bridge spanning the wide moat that protected the city. A long line of sand-colored asses, each tied to the animal ahead of it, clogged both the bridge and the Nergal Gate. Several of the agitated animals looked like they were about to sit upon their haunches, and the twin bags of pomegranates strapped to their backs swayed dangerously. An impatient crowd began to gather behind them. A few individuals pushed their way through the asses. Men shouted, oxen bellowed, and guards left their posts to bring order to the mess. Soulai used the commotion to slip unnoticed into the city.

His breathing quickened as he passed through the first massive wall. And despite the heat of the day, his skin felt chilled. Why am I doing this? Why am I walking back into the snare? It would be almost five years—more if he were punished—before he'd again see the outside of Nineveh.

Sunshine briefly warmed his head, then shadow cooled it as he passed through the second wall. His heartbeat doubled. He felt like an animal walking into a hunter's trap. One of the inner guards nodded respectfully, then squinted and looked closer. Soulai faked a casual glance away, suddenly remembering that he was dressed not only as a noble, but as Habasle. He would attract even more hunters. The determination that had filled him that very morning drained away. I'm not brave enough for this, he thought. He suddenly longed to just return Ti to the stable, take his beating from Mousidnou, and resume his work.

The marketplace was elbow to elbow with vendors hawking fragrant foods, women and children bargaining for the ingredients for the evening meal, and men trading stories and goods. Over the sea of dark heads, Soulai saw the scowling stone lamassu guarding the palace's western gate. At the top of the steps, in front of a large crowd, sat an old man. His yellow robe and halo of wild gray hair told Soulai it was Naboushoumidin. At least he'd done one thing right: He'd made it in time!

Looking around for a place to hide, he saw Jahdunlim enter the marketplace. The man sat on his horse, high above everyone else, searching the crowd. Soulai gasped, hurriedly slid off Ti, and pulled him behind some vendors' carts. As he squeezed in beside him, he noticed that the sweat had washed the dust from the stallion's coat. Once again it shone a brilliant gold and white—easy to spot! Unwrapping Habasle's robe, he tied it around the horse's neck. I don't know if I can do this, he thought again, as he drew his fingers through his hair. Above the clamor of the crowd he could hear that Naboushoumidin was just finishing a story.

Another figure appeared on the far side of the market-place. His blood-red attire and piercing stare were un-mistakable: the ashipu! He, too, was searching the crowd. Touching the cylinder seal that lay against his collarbone, Soulai had a new understanding of Habasle's tormented days. Even though it authorized great power, he considered taking it off.

At that moment the crowd groaned in unison, then ap-plauded. Naboushoumidin slapped his knees and waited for the chuckling and chattering to subside. When an expectant hush fell over the crowd, he spoke again.

"Now, this next story—my last one today—is for anyone in the audience who has ever been a friend or who has ever had a friend. I challenge you to turn to that person, look into their eyes, and learn whether or not you could trust that friend with your life. My story begins like this:

"Many, many years ago, a camel and a dog each became lost in the wilderness, and, as chance would have it, their miserable paths crossed. They were wary of each other at first, as strangers often are, but being unhappy together seemed better than being unhappy apart, so they agreed to travel on in the same direction. It didn't take long before the differences between the two animals became less bothersome, and the camel and the dog actually looked upon each other as friends.

"One day, however, it came to their attention that a lion was stalking them. So they bent their heads together to discuss what to do.

"'You have the sharp teeth,' said the camel to the dog. 'Snarl and growl and show him your fangs and maybe he'll leave us alone.'

"Now, the dog nodded to all that the camel was saying, but the whole time he was thinking only about

213

how he could save his own skin. 'All right,' he said to the camel, 'I'll run back and try to scare him away.' And off he went.

"But when the dog reached the lion, he didn't snarl or growl or show his fangs. Instead, he walked right up to the lion and boldly said, 'If you'll promise to spare my life, I'll make it possible—nay, I'll make it easy—for you to take the camel.'

"The lion, of course, agreed to this offer. The dog scampered right back to his friend, bragged about his bravery, and they traveled on. It wasn't too much farther until the pair came upon a wadi with very steep banks and only a trickle of water at the bottom, but as they were both very thirsty they decided to risk climbing down for a drink.

"'You may go first,' said the camel to his friend. 'After all, you saved both our lives.'

"'Oh, no,' countered the dog, without even a trace of guilt. 'You are much bigger and likely much thirstier. You go first.'

"So the camel bent his knees and took a tentative step down the bank. And you can just imagine what that deceitful old dog did. He gave his friend a shove and sent the creature tumbling end over end into the wadi. The lion rushed up and, seeing that the camel had been knocked senseless from the fall and was in no danger of escaping, turned to the dog. And ate him up first!"

Naboushoumidin sat back, watching the abrupt ending of his story sink in across the many upturned faces. A ripple of understanding cascaded into laughter. Friends elbowed each other, smiling good-naturedly, though a few blushed and hung their heads. Soulai felt his own face grow warm.

Another storyteller came from the palace to take Naboushoumidin's place and the chief scribe rose, stretched his neck, and started to turn away. Soulai panicked. He lifted his bandaged hand; then, afraid of attracting the wrong attention, dropped it. But the hasty movement caught Naboushoumidin's eye. He paused in his leaving to look back over his shoulder. Then he tossed a smile at the audience and nonchalantly walked down the steps to disappear into the crowd.

The other storyteller cleared his throat and began, leaving Naboushoumidin to meander past the baskets and behind the carts, until, noiselessly, he appeared at Soulai's side. Naboushoumidin's blue eyes widened in surprise. Then a toothy grin shot across his face. "A puzzle, a puzzle indeed," he exclaimed as he clasped his hands to his chest. "The prince Habasle is nowhere to be found. Now his slave appears, wearing his owner's robe and leading his horse." He leaned close. "I must say it doesn't bode well. You do have a good story, don't you?"

Soulai was taken aback. "No, no . . . it's not like that. Habasle's . . . sick," he stammered. "The ashipu's curse. An uridimmu—"

"*Where* is Habasle?" Naboushoumidin interrupted, his tone surprisingly sharp.

Soulai took a step away and fussed with the robe around Ti's neck. "A long way from here," he answered evasively. Something in the scribe's questions made him wonder whose side he was on. "And he's sick— very sick. There's a worm in his side and he's got the fever. He sent me to get the cure for the mad-dog curse."

"Hmm." Naboushoumidin rubbed his scraggly beard with his thick brown fingers. "Habasle wants something else from me when he has already stolen something from me."

Soulai's heart thudded so loud he could hardly hear. This is how the hare feels when the lion stalks near, he thought.

"The boy believes, perhaps," Naboushoumidin mused, "that because there are 268,492 tablets in the royal library that I would not miss one. But the skies are changing, King Ashurbanipal's astronomers tell me. The stars are realigning. So you can imagine my surprise when I am asked to bring forth the ancient tablets recording the moon's cycles—and find one missing. It is a small tablet, yet a particularly important one. In fact, as of this moment, it is the most important one."

An image flashed in Soulai's mind of Habasle clutching a flat clay object to his chest and rambling on about controlling the moon. The missing tablet! Habasle had stolen it.

The scribe's next words came dripping in honey: "You, perhaps, will know the location of this small tablet?"

Soulai shook his head. "I . . . I can't read," he mumbled. "I wouldn't know . . ."

The sound of coins jingling in a pouch beckoned him. "Silver has a way of clearing one's eyes, wouldn't you agree?"

Soulai swallowed. Staring at the bulging bag, he reluctantly nodded. For the second time that day he'd been offered enough silver to not only buy his freedom, but to most likely feed his family for a year. Enough silver to make him a man.

He looked nervously across the marketplace. A horse whinnied and Ti lifted his head to answer. Soulai caught his breath. The neighs wouldn't be noticed amid the noise—unless you were looking for a horse. As Jahdunlim was. And the ashipu as well.

Naboushoumidin pounced on Soulai's hesitation. "That's right. Eyes are everywhere. And not only are they looking for Habasle. They're looking for you, too. Rumor has it that you stole two of the palace's horses—ran away with them—though one, I have since heard, found its way home."

"I didn't steal them," Soulai protested. "Habasle took Ti and made me ride the other." Well, that wasn't exactly the truth, but he hadn't stolen them.

"And people have come to the library asking questions, interrupting my work. They left, but their eyes remain upon me." He shook his head. "So much trouble from two mere boys! And now you come pleading for my help."

Naboushoumidin spun the ivory cylinder seal on the thong around his neck. He studied the blue one around Soulai's.

"Does Habasle have my tablet?" he asked.

Soulai fidgeted. "I don't know," he mumbled. "Really, I don't." He looked up. "But I do know he's sick; he might even be dying. He needs your help."

"If he's dying, he's beyond anyone's help but the vultures'. And if he's sick he needs an asu."

Soulai sighed. He understood. The scribe hadn't gotten what he wanted and therefore he wasn't going to give him what Habasle needed. "Thank you anyway," he murmured. He began backing Ti along the wall. Where am I going to turn now? Soulai wondered.

"Describe his demeanor," Naboushoumidin commanded.

Soulai stopped. He looked down at his toes—funny, he was dressed as a prince and yet stood barefoot—and tried to remember everything. "He has the fever," he recounted carefully, "and a worm crawls in and out of the hole in his side—the one he got from the lance. And he's cold, and then he's hot. The spirits take over his tongue," he said, remembering Habasle's rantings at Dur Sharrukin. "The ashipu put an amulet carved of lapis lazuli in his pouch—Habasle said it was an uridimmu, a mad dog or mad lion, but I think the uridimmu already took his dog's form, because he got the sickness, too, and he's already dead and still Habasle's not right."

"One of his hunting dogs died? How?" The scribe was taking a keener interest now.

"A boar killed him when—"

"Oh, well, that is no sickness," he interrupted.

"But the dog was acting strange ever since we left the palace," Soulai argued. Maybe the man would help after all. "He was drooling and he wouldn't eat or drink—

even when he was standing in water. He wouldn't come near us, even when Habasle ordered it, except that when the boar was on top of Habasle, about to kill him, Annakum charged through and killed it. But just as Annakum was dying he tried to bite Habasle. I know he had the sickness. It's the curse, isn't it?"

Naboushoumidin scratched his beard again. "Where did all this take place?"

A small alarm sounded in Soulai's head. "On the road to Harran," he said truthfully.

"And how did you find a boar on the road to Harran?"

"Well, it was near the road. Ti was thirsty so we headed for the river. That's where the boars were. We killed two of them."

"Mmm." The scribe continued stroking his beard.

Panic kicked at reason again. Soulai considered running. "I think I'd better be going," he said nervously. "Do you . . . know the cure?"

The smile twitching on Naboushoumidin's face made Soulai very uneasy. "Aren't you the slave who wished Habasle dead?" he asked. "Why are you now risking your life to save him?"

Soulai just stared, frozen. This was the hare's final moment, he thought, too frightened to bound away. He couldn't even save himself.

Naboushoumidin clapped his hands loudly, making

Soulai jump. "Scribe!" he called into the marketplace. Several faces turned and Soulai shrank behind the cart, then straightened, for why would a noble be trying to hide?

A young scribe with a damp tablet of clay and raised stylus appeared. He glanced questioningly at the mismatch between Soulai's royal clothing and his bare feet.

"Now write this exactly," the gray-haired man said. "'So says Naboushoumidin, chief scribe to Ashurbanipal, king of all Assyria, to Habasle, son of Ashurbanipal. Drink down in its entirety milk in which a lizard has been boiled. Then say these words: He is long of leg, a fast runner. He does not need much food, is a poor eater. But to his teeth clings his seed; wherever he bites, he births a son. Away with him.'"

Naboushoumidin paused while the boy continued pressing the stylus into the clay. When the finished product was handed to him, he looked it over, took the stylus to correct a few strokes, then handed it back. He lifted his cylinder seal off over his head and rolled it across the bottom of the wet clay, leaving his signature pattern—an endless line of men carrying tablets into a library. Then he took a coin from his pouch, dropped it into the hand of the waiting scribe, and, taking back the tablet, dismissed him.

"Habasle reads better than he writes, so he should be able to understand this."

"Thank you," Soulai said. He unwrapped the robe from Ti's neck and carefully bundled it around the tablet.

"I can send someone with you, an asu if you'd like, to tend to the hole in Habasle's side."

Soulai shook his head. He was already searching the area for a place to get some goat's milk for Habasle, and measuring the distance to the Nergal Gate for a hasty escape.

"This cure, you understand," Naboushoumidin was saying, "is specific to the mad-dog disease. You say that the ashipu has set upon Habasle the uridimmu's curse. But I remind you that madness can take many forms." He smiled with a warmth that Soulai remembered from their talk outside the library. "You come to me again if you need me." With a nod, he backed away.

Soulai took a deep breath and, holding the robe with its valuable tablet close to his chest, led Ti into the bustling marketplace once more. He tried not to look around, but his eyes strayed. Fortunately he saw neither Jahdunlim nor the ashipu. When he spotted Mousidnou talking with a barley vendor, he ducked aside and hurried his steps, but the stable master didn't look his way.

A woman pulling two donkeys jostled her way in front of him and Soulai paused to let her pass.

"Well, the little bat returns in the daylight."

Soulai froze. The ashipu's long fingers gripped his shoulder and spun him around. Two other men, by the ashipu's order, tore the reins from Soulai's hands. A sharp blow to his stomach doubled him over. He fell to the ground, almost passing out, but through the nauseating fog managed to hear the ashipu exclaim, "What is this? Who are you?" A sandaled foot rolled him onto his back, exposing his face.

With his head reeling and vomit rising in his throat, there was no way Soulai could answer. He didn't have to, for the ashipu was already celebrating his triumph.

"Why, you're Habasle's slave. He's dead, isn't he? The curse has worked! You've got his clothes and I've got his horse. I knew it. The stars spoke of the death of a pretender to the throne and this proves it. It's over."

A heel slammed into Soulai's skull, once, twice, and a third blow landed on his throat. The clip-clop of horse hooves blended with the clamor of the marketplace, and then there was only the sun shining too brightly in his eyes and the vibration of many feet stepping around him.

HYSTERIA 2

If anyone noticed Soulai's misery, they soon forgot, for a shriek split the marketplace.

"He's dead!" a woman screamed. "My son's dead!" Through bleary eyes, Soulai caught a glimpse of her carrying the blood-covered body of a small child. The crowd closed around. Each curious newcomer asked the same question—"What happened?"—and received the same shrugged answer. But gradually, trickling back from the hysterical crying, came a murmur. "A lion!" "She said she saw a lion." The words leaped across the knots of people like a wildfire. "There's a lion loose here in the city." "A mad lion!" "A killer lion!"

Numbed beyond caring, Soulai let the news blaze around him. Then he heard another voice, as familiar as it was angry: Mousidnou's.

"Where in the name of Nergal have you been hiding your skinny ass?" he roared.

Soulai couldn't come up with a response, so he lay there, stupefied, until a hard kick landed between his ribs. He moaned and rolled over.

"Plagues! Looks like you've traveled through the underworld, boy. But where's the parti-color stallion? If he has but one hair out of place—one hair, mind you—I'll skin your worthless hide myself."

"I didn't steal him," was all Soulai managed to say. Then a horse's shrill whinny rent the air. "They're killing him. They're killing him," he cried, looking around wild-eyed.

Mousidnou tried to pull him upright. "Here, now," he scolded. "Sit up. I can't understand your whining. Who's killing what?"

"Ti. The ashipu is killing Ti. I was trying to save him but they took him—and I let him go. It's my fault."

The stable master looked around in vain. "Here, now," he said again. "Sit up." He tugged at Soulai once more. "Come out of the sun, boy."

Somehow Soulai managed to grab the fallen tablet before Mousidnou's beefy arm lifted him to his feet and steered him toward a shaded bench alongside the palace wall.

"Now," the man growled when Soulai had surrendered there in a slump, "where in the name of Nergal have you been for the better part of a week and where's my other horse? I'll not lose my head to Habasle because some thick-headed stable boy decided to go off on a gallop. You're lucky he hasn't come to the stables since his lion hunt."

"But he has," Soulai protested. He lifted the cylinder seal off from around his neck and handed it to Mousidnou. "He's the one who took Ti—after dark. Habasle said the ashipu was trying to kill him . . . and Ti, too, for a sacrifice and—"

"Wait! How did you get to be a part of all this? Did Habasle order you along?"

Soulai flushed. "I was worried about Ti. And Habasle was leaving so fast that I didn't have time to throw a rug on one of my ten. I just grabbed the chestnut and rode him without even a bridle. I wasn't stealing; I was looking out for Ti."

Mousidnou studied the carved blue pendant in his palm with a doubtful frown. A horse's piercing whinny made Soulai jump up again. He was certain it was Ti.

"That's him! We have to help."

Skeptical, the stable master cocked an ear. There was no subsequent call. "If the ashipu has chosen the horse for sacrifice," he said finally, shrugging his round shoulders, "then perhaps that is the best use for him. You heard the charioteer: he's been ruined for the hunt or for war." He looked past Soulai and sighed. "That stallion you favor isn't the first one to be cast aside as useless. And on a day like this, with every man sharpening his knife for battle, a quick slit across the throat sounds better than being left behind to rot within city walls."

"But Ti's not useless," Soulai argued. "He has Ninurta's mark—the hawk, you saw it—god of the hunt *and* of war. He'll prove himself; I know it. We have to stop the ashipu," Soulai pleaded.

"We?" Mousidnou repeated with a sneer. "Who has such power? The ashipu makes the stars move in the skies."

"Habasle says *he* can make the moon come and go."

"Then where is the all-powerful Habasle? If he cares so much for this horse, where is he?"

"Do you know a place called Dur Sharrukin?"

Mousidnou narrowed his eyes and nodded slowly.

"Habasle's waiting there; he was too sick to ride so he sent me." Soulai paused. "At least, I think he's still waiting. The ashipu said just now that Habasle's dead. He said he read it in the stars."

For what seemed like a long time Mousidnou stroked his beard and studied Soulai. Finally he said, "I guess I'm sorry to hear that. I had no love for the boy, but I feel less for that red-robed monster. He's got plans for all of us, some say."

The stable master's words surprised Soulai. "But

what if Habasle isn't dead?" he argued. "What if the ashipu is wrong? Naboushoumidin gave me the cure for his sickness—it's right here." He showed the tablet to Mousidnou, who gave it a cursory glance.

"And just what is my part to be in this?" the man asked.

"I need a horse...two horses, to bring Habasle back."

"Do I wear the look of an ox?" Mousidnou shouted. "Are you calling me stupid to my face? A stable boy steals two of my horses and sneaks off in the middle of the night and now I'm to give him two more and open the gate?" He shook his head in disgust. "If the ashipu says Habasle's dead, you can believe it. I'm not risking necks—of people or horses—to bring back a corpse. There's plenty of those on the way."

"What do you mean?"

"The Medes are challenging our borders. That's why everyone is preparing for war. The word is all over the city."

Soulai nodded. "That's what Habasle said. He made a drawing on a rock—"

"Everyone on watch," interrupted a palace runner. "A lion's loose from the zoo. One dead already."

Both Soulai and Mousidnou looked back toward the marketplace. The stable master became more agitated.

"Look here. I've horses to protect, if nothing else. So I suggest—no, I order—you to return to your work. You're to make up for the week's worth of chores another has had to do in your place. Now go. Go!"

Soulai moved toward the stable, shuffling at first, then picking up speed as he came up with a plan. He'd promised to save Habasle, and that's what he was going to do. Besides, Habasle had said he had something that the ashipu needed. He prayed that that would somehow save Ti.

The instant he entered the stable, Soulai retrieved two sets of tack, chose a horse from his ten, and set about readying him. He was just tightening the girth when Mousidnou came stomping down the aisle.

"What are you doing?" he demanded.

"Riding back for Habasle," Soulai answered firmly. "He's the king's son and it's my duty to save him."

Mousidnou scowled. "When was the last time you slept?"

"That doesn't—"

"You're in no condition to ride; you'll fall into the first moat and drown."

Soulai's fingers halted as he matched a determined stare with the stable master's.

"Plague it! You'd better be right," the man growled. Handing back the blue cylinder seal, he slapped his stomach and his demeanor changed. "It's been a great many years since this belly's been astride." He grinned at Soulai's stunned expression. "They're all getting ready to ride off to battle, thinking I'm too old, or too fat, maybe, to join them. Well, I'll show them. Now light a fire under your feet, boy," he roared, "and take the rug off this gray horse; he's a spine splitter. Find me an older one, with a soft back. That small gelding will do, the one with the chewed-off tail." He indicated the horse and Soulai quickly moved the rug and fastened the bridle.

Another horse was tacked for Habasle. "I'll bring back his body one way or another, I guess," Mousidnou said. "Now, you're sure the source of all this trouble is still at Dur Sharrukin?"

Soulai nodded. "He was inside the gatehouse of the main entrance when I left him. Here's the tablet with the cure against his sickness. Naboushoumidin said to boil a lizard in milk—I was thinking goat's milk would do—and make Habasle drink it."

A broad grin lit Mousidnou's face. "Gladly. Now," he said, a stern look extinguishing the smile, "*you* are to polish the hooves of your horses as well the ten on either side of yours. I want every mane combed out and every forelock and tail braided. They're going to war soon and they'll need to look like the king's chariot horses."

Stable boys peeked out from everywhere to watch Mousidnou balance on the edge of the water trough in order to climb onto his horse. While he was respected as a knowledgeable horseman, no one had ever before seen him ride. Astride and waving like a boy off on an adventure, he headed out of the palace. Just before he disappeared beneath the shadows of the lamassu, his final, oath-laden shout sent the stable boys back to their work.

All except Soulai, who waited alone in the courtyard, listening for Ti's whinnies. None came. I have to sneak away and look for him, he thought. But images of slashing claws and bloody fangs suddenly filled his mind—there was a lion loose in the city and he could be anywhere—he could be watching the stable at that very moment. Soulai felt his palms grow damp. He looked at the terraces above, tried to take a step toward them. Dusk was already falling. Maybe he'd have better luck finding Ti in the daylight. Hating himself for his cowardice, Soulai fled inside the stable.

WAITING IN 3 THE SHADOWS

He managed to polish maybe half a dozen hooves before a dizzy fog fell over him. With his head throbbing and his throat bruised and aching, Soulai fought to stay awake. But by nightfall, he was barely able to crawl to the spot near Ti's empty tether, where he collapsed. He sat, staring at it with tear-filled eyes, until his lids closed, and he felt himself plunging into a blackness that he both feared and embraced.

He awoke with a start. Lying there in the pitch dark, heart racing, he thought of the lion. Gradually he recognized the familiar sounds of the horses chewing and nickering, and he breathed easier. He was so thirsty, though, that he pushed himself from the floor and stumbled toward the courtyard.

The waxing moon painted the tiles silver and black. All the palace, in fact, was sharply defined by moonlit terraces and steps, and their connecting panels of shadow.

He hesitated in the doorway. His tongue was so dry it had swelled in his mouth. But wasn't that something over there in the darkness, a shadow moving within a shadow? For a long time he waited, squinting into the night and shivering. One, then two bats skimmed the trough's surface. All remained silent. Ti was out there, he scolded. If you can't brave the darkness for a drink of water, how are you going to come by the bravery to rescue him? But the nagging fear that one of the shadows had the shape of a lion held him captive inside the stable.

Heaving a sigh of misery, Soulai looked up at the stars. The great bird was there and yes, he had followed it back to Nineveh. The huge horse of stars galloped behind, just the way he'd galloped Ti. Probably to the stallion's death, he thought with a guilty pain. He dug his nails into his clenched palms. I'll search for Ti at daybreak, he promised.

Night finally gave way to morning, and Soulai, anxious to complete his morning chores so he could look for Ti, was the first in line with his grain basket. Although each step shot pain through his ribs, he hurried to deliver the barley hay, then began leading the horses to the watering trough.

Death was the topic there. Two more bodies had been found, the stable boys said, mauled by a mad lion. By the time Soulai had led the next horse to the trough, the count had risen to three. Then five, even six. Could it be the uridimmu? Habasle still had the blue amulet, he thought. But maybe the creature couldn't find Habasle. Maybe it had followed Soulai to Nineveh in the shape of a lion.

He was just tying the last horse and preparing to start his search when an unmistakable figure in a long red robe came prowling along the stable aisles. Hatred raged inside Soulai as he watched the ashipu stride up and down the rows of horses, obviously looking for something.

The man suddenly glanced in Soulai's direction. Recognition flickered across his face. "Where," he spat with disgust, "are the other horses?"

Soulai wanted to lunge for the man's throat, but he held himself back. "At the armory," he stated as evenly as he could. "Or the watering trough."

"And they are all returned here eventually?"

He forced himself to breathe. "By sunset."

"Tell me—and don't think I don't know who you are—is there any other place a horse would be taken in the palace . . . or the city? Outside the city, perhaps?"

Soulai's face remained expressionless as a flicker of hope took hold.

"If a horse required close attention," the man continued, "for example, from injury or illness, where would it be taken? And before you answer, remember who *I* am and what I can do to you." The threat ended in a guttural snarl, like a dog preparing to attack.

"All of King Ashurbanipal's horses are stabled here," Soulai responded. He ignored the threat; in fact, he had to restrain a smile. For why would the ashipu be searching for a horse when the only horse in which he was interested was Ti? Could it be that Ti had escaped him?

The ashipu loudly sucked in his breath and drew himself to his full height. "I require a red horse now, a blood-red one. And one black as the night. The particolor stallion that you and your master tried to steal from me was only the first of my sacrifices."

His black eyes fastened on Soulai's own. Sensing it was a test of some sort, Soulai forced himself to show neither fear nor surprise. Their stares held for a dozen pounding heartbeats. The ashipu finally exhaled, blowing a rancid wind into Soulai's face. Muttering a curse, he spun and strode out of the stable, his long red robe swishing about him. Soulai let out a long breath as well and allowed himself a brief shiver. Then he smiled. Ti was alive; he had to be. All I have to do now is find him.

Sneaking out of the stable as soon as he could, he searched those areas of the palace he thought might be big enough to hide a horse. Mindful that he was a slave, he tried to look like he was on important business; but he was so certain he'd discover Ti at the next turn that he had to purse his lips to keep from smiling. With light steps he hurried through the granary and the warehouse full of chariots, he poked through the debris-filled courtyard with the broken carts. Growing worried, he tiptoed through the kitchens and their storehouses of foodstuffs. Finally, dejected, he peeked inside two temples and even paused outside the gate to the harem. There were just so many places he couldn't enter.

The sky was deepening to lavender, and a dry chill had invaded the palace by the time Soulai returned to the stable. He fed and watered his horses, then slumped in the aisle opposite Ti's tether. His certainty that the stallion was alive had disappeared, and as he gazed at the empty tether it all but reached out and struck him. It's all my fault, he moaned. All my fault. Ti's dead because of me. He buried his head in his hands. Better that I'd never been born.

With the glimmering of the evening's first stars, the clip-clop of hooves announced an arrival. Mousidnou had returned; Soulai dutifully stood. The stable master rode right up to him, leading a horse on which Habasle, looking sick and disheveled, was hunched. Soulai noted his own slave tag resting prominently on Habasle's chest.

Before his mount had even come to a stop, Habasle slid to the ground with a pained groan. He took a step, handed the reins to Soulai, and fell forward into his arms. Soulai nearly collapsed from the unexpected weight. He struggled to drag Habasle away from the startled horses.

As Soulai helped him lie down, Habasle whispered, "Is he . . . ?"

Soulai swallowed. "I don't know," he murmured. "The ashipu and his men got him away from me yesterday. I'm sorry. But he was back this afternoon—the ashipu was—looking for a horse. Maybe—"

Habasle held up his hand. He nodded weakly. "Send for Naboushoumidin."

Soulai relayed the message to Mousidnou. The stable master groaned and stiffly twisted around, enough to lift a leg over his horse's rump. He dropped to the ground. Soulai feared he was going to crumple as well, but the man laid a hand on his lower back and slowly straightened. Complaining with every step, he tottered down the aisle.

While Habasle dozed and awakened in turn, Soulai untacked and fed the two horses. He was grooming the second one when Habasle mumbled something and beckoned him to his side.

"My identity. I want it back."

Soulai hesitated, then removed the blue cylinder seal from his neck and placed it in the open palm. Habasle had trouble pulling off the clay slave tag, so Soulai bent over to help. Before he slipped it over his own head, though, Habasle touched his arm.

"I didn't know if I could trust you back there."

Soulai felt the blood drain from his face. He nodded.

"You've proven yourself to me. I owe you my life."

As Habasle's eyelids drooped, Soulai fitted the clay tag around his own neck. I deserve nothing more than slavery for the rest of my miserable life, he sighed. He took up guard over Habasle until Naboushoumidin came running up the aisle in a manner that belied his years. Mousidnou trailed behind. The scribe's quick eyes surveyed the scene and he clapped his hands together. Curious as a child, he knelt and poked at the stained tunic. Habasle moaned. "Did you give him the cure?" Naboushoumidin asked.

Soulai looked at Mousidnou, who nodded.

The scribe sniffed and grimaced. "Worse than the wind of a sick dog. The worm may have been chased away, but its hole needs attention. I'll find an asu." As quickly as he had come, the man disappeared.

Half the night seemed to pass while they waited in silence. Mousidnou leaned his weight against the wall, grunting occasionally, though refusing to sit. Soulai knelt beside Habasle, longing for him to awaken and devise a plan to rescue Ti.

At last, Habasle stirred. "What night is it?" He searched blindly around him, finally settling a hand on one of his two pouches. When he fumbled with the opening, Soulai leaned forward and tugged it wide. Habasle reached in and carefully lifted out a palm-sized clay tablet. He cradled it to his chest. "What night is it?" he repeated. "What night?"

"It is the fifth of Tisri," Naboushoumidin answered loudly from down the aisle. The same bald-headed asu that had attended Ti's wounds followed uncertainly in his footsteps. "And the moon is straying from its calculated time."

"No," Habasle groaned. "It must be there, or—"

"—or there will be an invasion of a mighty city." Naboushoumidin finished the omen for him. "Yes," he continued, "the stars are spinning in the heavens, the warriors are gathering at the borders, the power is"—he cupped his hands together—"hanging like a nut from a tree and those who think they are the tallest are jumping to grab hold of it." He smiled as if enjoying a staged entertainment.

With great effort, Habasle straightened. He leveled a solemn stare at the gray-haired scribe. "How is my father preparing to battle the Medes?"

"By fasting in the darkness." A thinly veiled note of sarcasm colored the response. "The ashipu says he has read in the stars that King Ashurbanipal must prepare for war by fasting in seclusion: all day in the darkness, fasting, no meat; emmer but no meat." The familiar words rang in Soulai's ears, the same ones Habasle had mumbled at Dur Sharrukin. "Yes," Naboushoumidin said, "the ashipu is holding the reins to your father's kingdom."

"What's going to happen?" Soulai blurted.

"Ah! The power of the story: What's going to happen?" Naboushoumidin threw up his hands. "I don't know exactly—though I expect Habasle does."

Although all eyes turned upon him, Habasle's face remained mysteriously blank.

Naboushoumidin went on, more slowly. "I know that the ashipu wants to chase away the moon to prove his power, for if he can claim power over the stars, it is not a reach of his audience's imagination for him to claim power over the kingdom—"

"He can't!" Habasle hissed.

Naboushoumidin held up both hands. "I also know that he had wanted to sacrifice that horse of yours, the one with Ninurta's mark, to the god of war, but—"

"*Had* wanted?" Soulai asked.

Again the scribe raised his hands. "But power resides with he who possesses the knowledge."

Habasle removed his hands from the tablet and reluctantly offered it up. Naboushoumidin pounced. He quickly traced the symbols with his fingers, his lips moving silently as he read. Then he looked up, grinning. "He's planning a moonlit ceremony on the palace steps for two nights hence. But I believe there has been an error in his calculations."

"The moon will disappear on the sixth," Habasle said confidently. "Please, there is not much time. Tell us what you know."

Naboushoumidin shot a stern look at the still silent asu and squatted. He explained how the ashipu had come tearing through his library, searching for the tablets regarding the moon's actions. "This man had to have his tablet so badly that I simply made one for him. Give a child what he wants to stop his screaming, I say. Or what he thinks he wants." He grinned.

"What do you mean?" Mousidnou asked.

The scribe's blue eyes were twinkling. "I may have accidentally mistaken some of the dates and alliances on the tablet that I prepared for him. It wasn't easy making it look aged, but I have some skills that I haven't put to use in a long time." He looked at

Habasle. "But I'm afraid the moon is not the only actor who will fail to play his part for the ashipu." He paused, scanning the expectant faces in front of him. "His sacrificial victim is no longer available."

Soulai gasped. "Is Ti dead?"

Naboushoumidin smiled mysteriously. "He walks with the dead."

WALK WITH THE DEAD

Keeping to the shadows and out of the moon's glare, four figures crept from the stable, passed through empty courtyards, and traveled up and down stairs. Naboushoumidin led the way, the spring in his step revealing his excitement. Soulai followed at a less even gait, for Habasle's arm was flung heavily across his shoulders and the prince's unsteady legs threatened to topple them both. The asu lagged in the rear. At the outset, the asu had voiced an unwillingness to take part in the plot, until Naboushoumidin had shaken a finger at him and admonished that "King Ashurbanipal himself has asked us to look after his son." While those words had subdued the asu, they lit a proud smile across Habasle's face that even now seemed to help carry him along their trek. Mousidnou had stayed behind. He had offered to do anything he could to help, but the chief scribe suggested that he return to his room, and to his work in the morning, and listen for palace rumors.

Out of the darkness, twin flights of stairs appeared before them. One led up to a courtyard that surrounded the harem; the other led down to a small landing that in turn opened onto another flight of narrow stairs. Naboushoumidin darted down the second flight.

Even before the heavy stone door at the bottom was eased open, Soulai suspected what it hid: a tomb. Dread stirred in his belly. More death. Naboushoumidin cautioned them to silence with a finger to his lips, then slipped through the gap. After a few breathless moments, a small flame illuminated the entry. Habasle, Soulai, and the asu crept into the tomb.

The dry air stung their nostrils. Faint odors arose, some pungent, some sweet and lingering. Still another smell, a sharp one, assaulted them as Naboushoumidin smeared a thumbprint of black grease across each of their foreheads. "To fend off the spirits," he whispered.

The light from his lantern danced across a wide, vaulted passage. Stone sarcophagi, partially submerged in the hard earth, lay in orderly rows on either side of a brick walkway. Dust clouded the intricate inscriptions on their lids. As Soulai proceeded, large, shadowy shapes loomed out of the darkness. He recognized them as chariots resting on empty shafts. A few more steps

244

and he discovered rotting harnesses surrounding crumbling bones—the skeletons of horses, he realized with a sudden queasiness.

A tremulous nicker from the darkness startled him. The spirit of a dead horse! But it couldn't be. Its familiarity tugged at his senses. It had to be Ti!

The chamber ended with two short passageways extending left and right. Peering down one, Soulai saw stacks of lances, shields, and bows, and quivers stuffed with arrows. At the entrance to the other, two carved ivory chairs waited like upright skeletons. Habasle collapsed into one, holding his side. Naboushoumidin shot a stern look at the asu, who immediately bent over Habasle and began probing his wound.

The nicker sounded again, and, as the scribe set about lighting lanterns, Soulai peered down the blackened passageway until he gradually made out the form of his beloved stallion. The horse had been hobbled and blindfolded, and thick cloths wrapped his hooves. The head, unseeing, was lifted in their direction.

Soulai walked straight to the bound horse, knelt, and removed the blindfold. Ti shook the forelock out of his eyes, then laid his head in Soulai's lap, letting out a great sigh. Although there were no marks on him, he seemed near death. Trying to control his worry, Soulai stroked Ti's brow while listening to the old scribe.

"I found him in the farthest reaches of my library last night," Naboushoumidin was explaining, "hobbled and blinded like so. I suspect the ashipu hid him there. But you know how I feel about beasts in my library."

Habasle responded with a brief, bitter smile. Soulai knew he was remembering Annakum.

"The hoof cloths were my own addition," the scribe went on, "so that I could move him here without anyone hearing. It was before the moon rose; I don't believe anyone saw."

He fell silent. An invisible power had been growing, emanating from Habasle. The two men seemed to recognize it, and, in fact, seemed to wait for it to direct their lives. As ill as he was, or maybe because of it, Habasle's eyes began to burn with a determined fire.

"What does my father want me to do?"

"Is the king still fasting?" Naboushoumidin asked the asu, and when the bald man nodded, he continued. "As he's yet captive in his own darkness, I'm not sure he could tell you what to do."

There was a pause before Habasle posed a second question. "What do *you* think I should do?"

Naboushoumidin laced his fingers and stretched his arms over his head. "The horse, Ninurta's messenger, is rightfully back in your hands," he said, "as well as a tablet—perhaps not so rightfully—endowing mastery over the skies. With the ashipu believing you are dead, you also possess an element of surprise—the hunter's most valuable asset." He spread his palms and bowed grandly. "Thus, I say it is up to you, Habasle, to write the next chapter."

"To make my mark," Habasle murmured thoughtfully. "The moon disappears tomorrow night. Do you think we can hide here for one more day?"

Naboushoumidin nodded. He pointed to a pouch resting beside a pitcher. "I've brought food and water for you, though I couldn't provide anything for the horse without being found out."

Soulai looked up. He saw that Habasle sat straighter, that he no longer clutched his side. Their eyes met. "Return to the stable," Habasle commanded. "Seek out Mousidnou and only him, but tell him nothing. Just request as much hay and grain as you can carry in my pouch"—he dumped the remaining contents onto the floor and handed it to over—"and make certain that no one sees you or follows you—"

"Perhaps," interrupted Naboushoumidin, "perhaps I should go. Should anyone find us out, we'll pay with our lives."

Habasle shook his head, his solemn gaze never leaving Soulai's face. "I trust him," he said. "No one will find us. Now go."

Caught up in the power of the moment, Soulai lifted Ti's head from his lap and stood. "He needs water, too," Soulai suggested as he fit the pouch over his shoulder. It occurred to him that he had said these same words on their first meeting. Habasle must have remembered, too, for a smile flickered across his lips. He spoke sternly, however, as a master must to his slave. "We'll share the water that is already here for now. But you shall find a bucket and carry more from the trough."

The asu turned from attending Habasle's wound. "There's a lion loose in the city, you know. A mad one, they say."

"A mad lion?" Habasle repeated with interest. He reached for his other pouch, and the asu quickly handed it to him. Digging through it, he pulled out the blue amulet depicting the uridimmu. A shiver ran up Soulai's spine. "And you wanted to throw it in the river," Habasle said. With a free hand, he dismissed Soulai.

Soulai gave Ti one more caress and turned to go. Silence followed him as he tentatively made his way toward the tomb's entrance, silence except for Habasle's parting order: "Be careful."

With no lantern to light his path, he had to shuffle, arms outstretched and toes feeling for the bricks. When

248

his fingers finally touched the stone door, he let out a sigh of relief, then squeezed through the narrow opening. The chill night air prickled his skin—he hadn't realized how warm it had been inside the tomb. Turning, he pushed against the heavy door, which made such a loud scraping sound as it was closing that he could only push a little at a time. At last he tiptoed up the steps, and proceeded around the shadowy edges of the first courtyard's barren expanse.

The escaped lion could be padding through this same courtyard, he thought, and at the same instant: for once in your life, don't be a coward. Breaking out in a nervous sweat, he carefully measured the distance from one doorway to the next and crept through the darkness.

But the lion was not the night's only predator. Soulai knew that palace eyes were always watching from somewhere and so he took a particularly circuitous route back to the stable. He walked past the kitchens and angled toward the room he had once shared with the other stable boys. Hugging the walls, he crossed another courtyard, headed for the library, then circled back toward the stable by another series of courtyards and steps.

Only when he descended into the warm, fragrant atmosphere of the stable did Soulai realize he had been holding his breath. A hand grazed his shoulder and he jumped, gasping. It was Mousidnou.

"I have the hay and grain," he whispered. He tipped his head toward a sheaf of hay on which rested a pile of grain.

"How . . . how did you know?" Soulai stammered.

"The ashipu just left here. Woke me from a dead man's sleep to ask about the parti-color stallion. I told him I hadn't seen the damned horse in a week. After he left, I couldn't find you, or Habasle, so I figured the two of you had something to do with it. Say, what's that on your forehead?"

Soulai rubbed at the grease mark, trying to decide how much he should tell.

"I'll help you carry the feed," the stable master said. "Where are you keeping the stallion?"

Dropping his hand, Soulai studied the oiliness on his fingers while contemplating his answer. This was Mousidnou, who had ridden back to rescue Habasle; surely he could be trusted. But that brought back Habasle's words: *I trust him. No one will find us.* Soulai shook his head. "I can't say," he said. "I have to take it alone."

Mousidnou raised himself up and Soulai cringed, expecting a blow. But the man only shrugged, looking almost hurt. "Here you are, then," he said gruffly, taking the pouch from Soulai's shoulder and stuffing the grain and hay into it. "You'd better fetch him some water, too. I've hidden a bucket behind the large olive tree near the well. Now move your ass. I'm not staying awake all night for palace gossip."

Soulai nodded respectfully, backed down the aisle and out of the stable. He paused in the doorway to scan the courtyard.

The air hung still. Muted voices from the palace kitchens drifted through the darkness. Soulai saw a bat skim the trough for a quick drink. Footsteps sounded and he spotted a guard patrolling the walled terrace, the butt of his spear thumping with each step. Soulai waited for him to pass, then slipped across the courytard.

The skin bucket was nestled behind the potted olive tree as Mousidnou had said. Soulai dropped the bulging pouch and carried the container to the trough. He laid it in the water, but the water was too shallow; he'd have to pull more from the well. That wasn't good. The ropes rubbing on the wheels would surely make noise. He looked around again, saw no one, and reached for the main rope. The first tug let out a loud squeak. He tried coaxing the rope along slowly, and though this softened the sound, it lasted much longer. After an eternity, he felt the weight of a full bucket rise. The rope squeaked louder. Nothing to do but keep pulling, steadily.

"What are you doing there?"

Heart leaping, Soulai looked up at the guard leaning over the wall.

"Getting some water for a horse," he croaked.

"Why don't you bring him out to the water?" The voice sounded suspicious.

"He's been injured," Soulai answered truthfully. "Mousidnou told me to fetch water with this bucket."

The guard hesitated, then seemed satisfied, for he returned to his thumping strolling, though Soulai noted he adjusted his path closer to the wall and frequently glanced over it. In fact, when Soulai tipped one of the well's buckets into his smaller one and turned to leave, the guard was leaning against the wall watching him. Feeling self-conscious, Soulai picked up the pouch and, rather than leaving the courtyard by the steps, turned and reentered the stable. He waited inside, nervous, biding his time like a mouse in its hole. He counted the guard's thumping, peeking out often enough to see the stars shift in the skies. Time was passing. Surely Habasle and Naboushoumidin would be wondering where he was. Ti, poor Ti, who had passed more than two days with nothing to eat, would be growing hungrier and thirstier by the moment.

The thumping faded and disappeared. Soulai counted to a hundred and when the thumping still hadn't returned, he cautiously stepped outside. He waited, listening. The courtyard and the walled terrace above it remained empty.

Still on the alert, he tiptoed toward the steps. He was on the third one when a hand brushed his back, startling him into a loud gasp. He turned to respond to Mousidnou but instead came face-to-face with the ashipu. A sinister smile twisted the man's features. When he spoke, the deep voice could have been one of the tomb's evil spirits.

"You have something I want."

Illogically, the hay-and-grain-filled pouch came to Soulai's mind and he involuntarily placed a hand over it.

"Not that, you fool. The stallion, the parti-color stallion. Where is he?"

Soulai shook his head. Despite his trembling, he had to feign ignorance.

The ashipu grabbed him and, with fingers as strong as iron, dragged him down the steps and back across the courtyard. The skin bucket slipped from Soulai's hands, spilling its water across the tiles. The man strode straight for the well and shoved Soulai against it so hard that the brick edge cut him across the middle, doubling him over. A dank odor splashed across his face as his head dangled in the void. The point of a knife poked beneath his ribs.

"Where is the stallion?" the evil voice hissed again.

This was it, Soulai thought. The moment when he had to be brave enough to choose death rather than surrender to the enemy. He pictured the bas-relief carvings surrounding the library, the panels showing the citizens of the captured city boldly jumping into the river and drowning. He remembered the fishes nibbling at the bloated bodies. But Ti was worth it. Then he jammed an elbow backward into the ashipu, leaned farther into the well, and dove into the darkness.

ARIGHTING 5

Water closed over his face and ran its fingers around his body, pulling him down. The sharp coldness forced a gasp from his lungs and more water poured into his mouth, burning his nose and choking his throat. His legs flailed above his head, frantic but useless. Something solid grazed his shoulder, then it slid away as he tumbled. His fingers became tangled in the knotted rope, the hay-filled pouch; his toes found the well's skin buckets. He searched for a hold and managed to break the surface. Coughing and gasping, he clung to the rope with both hands, trying to breathe in enough air. The rope began vibrating in his fists, and then he was falling down through the water again, the rope limp in his hands, more rope falling in coils around him.

The buckets weighed him down; the snaking ropes noosed his feet. Soulai kicked at them again and again. His head bobbed out of the water and his fingers found the well's wall, slick with its bitumen coating. He clawed at it, trying to catch hold, but sank. Blindly he splashed, grasping for the slimy wall and feeling it slide past his fingers over and over—until the tip of one finger caught a shallow crevice and somehow he managed to pull himself out of the water just long enough to suck in a chestful of air. That unbalanced him, he lost his grip, and he found himself again submerged.

For a punishing eternity, until the tips of his fingers were torn raw, Soulai managed to stay alive one gulping breath at a time. Invariably he lost his grip and plunged into the water again, but slowly the panic ebbed and he began to remember where the saving crevice was and to hang there quietly when he found it, though the water lapped right at the level of his nose and the threat of suffocation stiffened his limbs. Gradually, too, he was able to work his free hand across the wall and, when he found another crevice, to mold his fingers into it.

He hung there, cheek pressed to the slick bitumen, arms spread like a bat's wings, shivering. Numbed, he took only shallow breaths, fearful of losing his balance. He briefly thought about what had happened that night and what he needed to do, but the stupefying cold dulled his mind and the simplest of tasks—hanging on—became his sole focus.

But at some point, filtering through his unending

pain, came an awareness of a subtle change inside the well: He could dimly make out his pale, cramped fingers. With his cheek still flush to the wall, Soulai thankfully welcomed the morning light. The slapping of sandaled feet in the courtyard above signaled the stable boys coming to their work. His heart beat a little faster as he waited, listening for the sound that might lead to his rescue. Finally, there it was: the clopping of hooves. The first horses were being led to the trough, there'd be—

"Hey! Where's the rope? What's happened?" Voices echoed down to him; he didn't dare look up. A head must have been thrust into the well, for the next voice was clearer. "I think someone's fallen in. Hey! Hurry along, there! Get another rope." The commotion built. More heads must have surrounded the opening, for the voices mingled and reverberated louder. And then a heavy rope slapped atop his head, dangled down his back. Soulai knew he had to let go, though his hands were frozen in place and he was shivering such that real movement seemed impossible. The rope danced, banged his head, then flopped against his face. With a gasping lunge, he released his hold. He grabbed onto the rope, lost his balance, and went underwater. He came up spluttering, still holding onto the rope with all the strength he could muster, then grabbing it with the other hand. It tightened and Soulai could feel himself lifted from the water, his body hanging limp and dripping below his clenched fists.

The height grew dizzying, but he closed his eyes and concentrated on hanging on. Then arms were reaching for him, under him, lifting him farther out of the well, up and over its sharp brick lip.

"By the rivers of the underworld, how did you get down there?" It was Mousidnou, hands planted on his knees, bending over, frowning with genuine concern. "You and you," he was ordering brusquely, "carry him into the stable. And you two, start fishing for that broken rope. There's a thousand of the king's horses waiting to drink."

More dizziness as he was carried through the air. The cushion of barley hay soft against his back as he was plopped onto a pile and rubbed all over with cloths. His teeth chattered incessantly; he couldn't stop them. The wet tunic was yanked over his head; a clean, dry one was somehow fitted back over it. He was powerless to help.

When the stable boys were chased away to do their work, Mousidnou leaned over him. "What's going on here?"

"The ashipu—he tried to—make me tell him—where

Ti is," Soulai chattered. "I didn't—get the food—to him. All night—he's hungry."

"Well, where in the name of Ninurta is he?"

Soulai rolled his eyes up at the man. His teeth moved but his lips didn't.

The stable master sat back with a grunt. "I know, I know. You can't tell *me* either. Well, I'm through breaking my ass to help you and Habasle play your games. Get back to your work." He got to his feet and walked off.

Soulai watched him lumber down the aisle. He used the time to rub the warmth of life into his legs. When he felt able to walk, he quickly bundled some hay inside his discarded tunic and slipped out of the stable.

With the sun yet hidden below the gray sky, only slaves and guards, cooks and washerwomen hurried around the palace. Few nobles would be awake, so Soulai ducked his head and boldly strode into the bustle.

But leaving the commotion to strike out in the direction of the harem and its ever-vigilant guards was another matter. For a long time Soulai knelt over his hay-filled tunic, pretending to secure the load. Out of the corner of his eye he watched the guard closest to him march back and forth. When the man neared the far point of his circuit, Soulai dashed down the stairway to the tomb.

The stone door was closed and he leaned against it, panting. Dare he enter? Keeping a watchful eye above, Soulai pushed his weight into the door. It didn't budge. He groaned and sank his forehead against it. Then, taking a couple of deep breaths, he shoved his shoulder into the door again, willing it to move. And gradually, though it rasped a complaint, it opened. Soulai squeezed through the gap. There was no sound of footsteps, outside the tomb or within.

Today the vault's stifling heat felt good and his limbs began to unknot. The sliver of light showed the lantern sitting in its niche beside the door. He lit it, held it high, and walked into the darkness. He expected to hear something, a greeting or command from Habasle, but there was only silence. And when he reached the tomb's end, he found it empty. They'd left without him! Did they think he'd betrayed them?

Or . . . maybe the ashipu had found them and they'd been killed! Where was Ti? With a chill, he peered down the short arm of the vault to where the stallion had been hobbled. Panic shot through him as he made out the horse's motionless form on the brick floor.

Not wanting to believe his eyes, he moved closer. The horse had been blindfolded again and a short rope had been knotted through his halter and snugged around his nose. Soulai fell to his knees. He worked feverishly to pull off the blindfold and untie the muzzle. To his relief, Ti blinked; he was still alive. All the while talking to him, Soulai unfastened the hobbles and removed the cloths from Ti's hooves. But the stallion didn't try to get up. He just lay there, neck outstretched, barely breathing.

"Ti," Soulai whispered. "It's me." He caressed the horse's cheek.

The stallion blinked a few times, then rolled his gold eye toward Soulai. In one glance it seemed to say, It's no use.

"No," Soulai found himself responding. "Look, I've brought food. And there must be some water left here."

The eye rolled back and closed. With a gasp, Soulai lifted the lantern higher. The way the light flickered across the white marking of Ninurta made it appear that the hawk's wings fluttered and slowed. Fearfully, he touched Ti's shoulder. The stallion was still warm. "No," he commanded. He set down the lantern and began kneading the horse's muscles, pushing and pulling at the skin. Imagining that the body beneath his hands was his clay, Soulai willed it to come to life. He stroked Ti's neck, rubbed his forehead, tugged gently on his soft nostrils. And all the while he prayed.

Ti lifted his head. Soulai found what was left of the water and shoved a bowl toward him. The horse drank.

261

Before Ti could lower his head again, Soulai moved behind him and supported him with his own body. He cupped a handful of hay beneath the muzzle and while Ti ate he continued rubbing his hands over the horse.

As he stroked the stallion, Soulai noticed a richly colored rug that hadn't been in the tomb the evening before. The lantern showed that the weavers had outdone themselves. Wool as white as clouds alternated with bands of sky blue and a purple the color of amethyst. A deeper Tyrian purple dyed the fringe that hung more than a hand's width on each side. Lying beside the rug was a beautifully tooled bridle decorated with white tassels. Its iron bit, unblemished, had yet to rest in a horse's mouth. And springing up from the crown was a huge, regal white plume. These were the fittings of a royal horse charging off to war; Soulai remembered them from the carvings around the library. Habasle was preparing Ti for battle.

The idea sat differently with him now. He'd found the bravery to challenge death—and that had freed him from his past. In his father's eyes, and in his own, he knew he was a man. Naboushoumidin's words came back to him: *Each one of us has a destiny that must be pursued wholeheartedly, yea though it brings death early, for death will surely come eventually.* Soulai fingered the gold and silver mane, and, though he couldn't help wincing, he pictured Ti prancing across a battlefield outfitted in such regal tack. He could accept it now. It was the stallion's true destiny.

Bittersweet images kept crowding his mind until the tomb's warmth and his own weariness lulled him to sleep. It was Ti's explosive snort that awoke him. He came to groggily, but straightened to attention when he saw that the horse was staring with evident alarm into the darkness stretching between them and the stone door. He couldn't see anything, but he could hear it: Someone was inside the tomb with them. And approaching.

Recalling the weapons stashed in the opposite arm of the tomb, Soulai retrieved a spear and a knife. Just as he was crouching beside Ti once more, a series of grunts sounded from the void.

His hair stood on end. They hadn't escaped death yet. The lion was in the tomb—the mad lion. Maybe the uridimmu! Ti was frantically trying to scramble to his feet and Soulai threw a leg across his back and rose with him. Ti pawed the ground, fretting at the unseen predator.

And then it was seen. Padding out of the darkness came a black-maned lion, tail swishing, nonchalant and confident. It paused to sniff at some bones, batted at them with a huge paw, then continued along the brick path. The lantern's small flame shone in the cat's cold yellow eyes. It stared at its prey, coolly appraising them, then strolled into the passageway opposite. Dropping to the floor, it studied horse and boy.

Ti pranced and spun and it was all Soulai could do to stay atop him, crouched as he was to avoid the low ceiling. But there would be no plunging to the exit, for the lion was sure to attack. Somehow, above Ti's snorts, Soulai detected another presence in the tomb. Before he had time to even consider it, the ashipu, great robe flapping, leaped from the darkness at them. Shouting a curse, the ashipu grabbed for Ti's halter. The stallion pinned back his ears, reared up, and struck out with his hooves. Soulai was fumbling with the spear as the man staggered backward, holding his shoulder.

The lion, which had been watching the melee with keen interest, spotted a victim. In three lightning-quick bounds it was upon the fallen man. An agonized shriek was immediately drowned by snarling. Soulai's heart banged wildly. Struggling to control Ti, he coaxed him past the attacking lion. They could escape!

But in no more than two strides, Soulai found himself pulling on the lead rope and turning the horse back. He clenched his jaw. He had one more thing to prove, and so did Ti: They didn't run from lions.

The horse pricked his ears as Soulai urged him toward the fight. With a frightened snort, he spun away. Soulai wrestled him around to face the lion. Ti tossed his head and pawed the ground nervously, but held his place. Ever so surely, Soulai closed his legs around the horse. He sat deep and loosed the reins, letting Ti choose. A confidence seemed to settle over the stallion; Soulai felt the powerful haunches gather beneath him. With barely a nudge then, he positioned Ti sideways, and the horse boldly swung close to the lion. Soulai raised his spear, eyed the savage lion's back and, with all his strength, drove the blade in. Another chilling scream filled the tomb. The creature stumbled away from the body of the ashipu and fell.

Ti was suddenly beyond containment. He reared once, twice, his hooves narrowly missing the ashipu's body each time they landed, though the man didn't move. The horse shook his head furiously. Soulai needed a bridle. Cautiously, he slid from Ti's back and, stretching at the very end of the lead rope, managed to grab the feathered headstall. He tucked it under his arm and, snapping the rope to try and quiet the stallion, led Ti past the rows of sarcophagi to the stone door.

The stallion, brimming with triumph, stamped his feet. It was all Soulai could do to slip off the halter and quickly replace it with the bridle. A restless champing sounded in the vault as Ti mouthed the new bit. He arched his neck and the huge white feather stood erect from his proud crest. Soulai smiled. Leaning his shoulder into the heavy door, he pushed on it until it scraped open far enough to let Ti through.

He was shocked to find that dusk had fallen. At least he thought it was dusk. But there was something different about this evening; an eerie coppery glow bathed the walls of Nineveh. He looked up at the sky. The moon, round and full, shone blood red.

MAKING 6 HIS MARK

A muted roar that surged and ebbed sounded in the distance. Soulai tipped his head and listened, then led Ti up the steps, hooves clattering loudly. The noise was coming from outside the palace, in the direction of the marketplace, and though he was near to collapsing, he marched the head-tossing Ti across the limestone courtyards now awash in the odd, coppery hue. As they neared the palace's western gate, the one outside which Naboushoumidin often told his stories, Soulai heard someone making a speech.

"As the sharqi drops from the sky and sweeps across the land, breaking into bits all that it encounters, so shall we gallop, scattering the Medes before us. As the lightning splits the tree, separating leaf from limb and limb from trunk, so shall the lightning of our swords separate hand from arm and head from body. As the scorpion stings the heel, inflicting great pain and suffering on its victim, so shall the army of Assyria sting the heels of the fleeing Medes, again and again and again!"

It was Habasle, Soulai knew, even before he peeked through the parted gate. The prince stood wrapped in a regal new robe of white and purple and blue, and, though he supported his weight on the upright staff of his spear, he vigorously punched the air with a fist to the rhythm of his words. Naboushoumidin stood to the side, hands clasped to his chest. Ringed by flaming torches, the marketplace was filled with people who turned their awestruck faces alternately between the speaker and the reddened moon.

"For eight months," Habasle shouted, "since the days of winter, the gods have laid forth their plans for Nineveh's victory. To those who were looking, they revealed themselves in the heavens. And to those who would learn, they unlocked the tablets' secrets. And Ninurta himself, the great and glorious Ninurta, god of the hunt, god of war, god of victory, has sent to me as his own messenger a stallion that—"

Succumbing to the spirit of the moment, Soulai impulsively trotted Ti through the gate. The crowd roared. The horse responded by arching his neck and rolling his deep gold and pale blue eyes. The white plume tossed gloriously upon his crest, the tassels danced madly. Held in check by the new bit, Ti pranced in place.

Soulai handed the reins over to Habasle. Then, without speaking, Soulai turned and faced the crowd. He waited at Ti's shoulder and, behind his back, locked his hands and offered them as support to a flawless mount.

A whispered thank-you met his ears. Soulai felt the weight of a sandaled foot on his palms, steadied himself, and in the next instant, the weight was lifted and Habasle sat astride Ti. As the crowd cheered, Soulai stepped away.

"On the wings of Ninurta, the Assyrian army will fly—"

The gold-and-white stallion reared and pawed at the night sky, holding his huge body aloft for so long that he looked ready to soar into the blackness and challenge even the great horse made of stars.

As the hooves scraped upon stone, the crowd fell suddenly silent. Thousands of eyes looked past Habasle and Ti, and Soulai turned as well. A retinue of noblemen came marching from the palace in solemn pairs, the ones at the front dispersing clouds of fragrant smoke from stone bowls, and the ones behind holding aloft their own flaming torches. The billowing smoke turned as orange as the moon. Its thick fingers curled around the feet of the lamassu, drifted down the steps, and threaded through the crowd, and the marketplace took on an otherworldly glow.

Murmured awe announced the appearance of an unearthly god. If it was not Ashur himself, king of all the gods, it was his divine messenger and representative in human form. Firelight glistened off the gold adorning his neck, his ears, his arms. The body was old, but held rigidly erect in its heavy robe fringed with tinkling glass beads. The god-king walked straight toward the crowd, looking neither left nor right, one arm resting on the ivory hilt of a sword angling from the gilt sheath fastened at his hip.

Soulai stepped back into the shadows as the figure strode forward. Like the crowd, Ti became silent as his rider slid from his back to bow with respect. Habasle straightened—Soulai knew it had to hurt—and summoned a regal bearing that matched that of the older man. Ashurbanipal laid a hand on Habasle's shoulder, then turned and spoke to the crowd.

"Ishtar," he said loudly, "protectress of our city, has come to me in my fasting." Not a breath sounded from the marketplace. "In my dream, from each of her shoulders hung a quiver full of arrows. She advanced toward me and spoke to me like a mother. 'Thou hast asked for victory,' she said. 'Let thou knowest that where thou art, I am also.'"

An approving murmur rippled through the audience.

"And I spoke to her as a worthy son. 'Can I go with thee where thou goest, O sovereign of sovereigns?' And she answered. 'Stay thou in the temple consecrated to me; eat thy food, drink thy wine. For I will go out to the battle and I shall accomplish my work. Vengeance on thine enemies shall be mine.'"

With these last words, Ashurbanipal pulled his sword free and thrust it high into the air. The ripple of applause exploded into a riotous cheer.

Ti, who up until now had stood motionless, craned his neck around. Soulai had a distinct feeling that the horse was looking for him. Even from the short distance, he could read the uncertainty in Ti's eyes. Did Soulai really want him to take part in this battle? they seemed to ask. Did Soulai really think he was brave enough to serve the gods?

Soulai smiled. With pride filling his chest, he nodded, then flung his arms in the air, motioning Ti away. The gold-and-white stallion with the mark of Ninurta tossed his head and reared once more, and the crowd cheered wildly.

The shadow was sliding from the moon now, returning it to its silvery state. Sensing that his part was played out, Soulai slipped back through the gate and into the palace. He didn't know which way to turn. An odd feeling made him touch his chest, and he frowned at discovering that his clay tag was missing. But how and when? In the well? Battling the lion?

Footsteps approached through the darkness. "Wait! Stop!" Soulai looked over his shoulder. It was Habasle, hobbling as fast as he could, holding his side.

As ordered, Soulai waited. He watched his owner approach. There was a different look to him, a happy confidence that lessened his swagger.

"Did you hear?" Habasle asked between gasps. "Did you see? I beat the ashipu to his own prediction." He looked up at the full moon and grinned. "You know what I think happened? His own curse got him. Look," he spread his arms to indicate the near empty courtyard, "he's nowhere to be found. And do you know what else has happened? I'm leading my father's entire army into battle. On Ti. He says Ishtar has spoken to him and assured Nineveh of victory." He thrust his fist into the air again. "How is that for leaving your mark? We ride at dawn to slay every last one of those Medes and be home before the rains come."

A tired smile creased Soulai's face.

"That's it?" Habasle exclaimed. "Nothing to say?"

"Take care of Ti. He made his own mark tonight," he said, thinking of the stallion's bravery.

Whether Habasle heard his request, Soulai didn't

know, for his master was busy untying a bag at his waist. Finally he handed it to Soulai. "Here," he said. "There's more than enough to buy your freedom."

Stunned, Soulai felt the weighty bag settle in his upturned palm.

Habasle turned to go back to the crowd, still clutching his side. "I suppose I could take you with me," he said, "but you don't follow orders." He hurried off, close to skipping with his hitching gait. "And you can't swim," he hollered back in the growing dark.

Soulai's smile widened. He watched the boy whom he'd once hated rejoin the revelry, then continued his meandering walk. He felt lost, shapeless as a lump of clay. In the past, he'd always turned to his clay when he needed to work something out, but those days seemed gone. He thought briefly about going to the stable, but he couldn't bear to look at the empty tether and know that Ti might never return to it. So his journey led him aimlessly up and down steps and across terraces and past the room he had shared when he first arrived at Nineveh. He peeked inside. It was empty; they were all on the palace steps, no doubt. He ambled past the kitchens, inhaling the aroma of fresh loaves.

Sometime later he found himself standing outside the royal library. Beneath the bright moonlight the masterful carvings of war leaped from the building in stark relief. There were the men on camels . . . the people jumping into the water . . . the horses galloping across the battlefield. Soulai reached out and stroked the forehead of one of the horses.

"What will happen to the stallion, you are wondering." The voice made him jump. It was Naboushoumidin, who emerged from the shadows to stand at his side.

Soulai nodded. He pressed his fingers hard to the stone.

"He is pursuing his rightful destiny. As you are yours."

"Mine?" Soulai croaked.

"Habasle has set you free, yes?"

Soulai felt his head nod again.

"And so your own feet have carried you here, to the carvings, a place of great significance. I remembered from talking with you that you see our city, and especially our horses, through the eyes of an artist. And I have long wondered if your hands can follow your heart." The scribe stepped close to the panels and reverently laid his palms over the raised images. "Do you realize that years and years after your tongue and mine and those of Assyria's next twenty kings are but dust, these scenes will continue to tell the stories?" He looked over his shoulder. "And there is yet another story—an important one—that needs to be told, don't you agree?"

At first Soulai didn't follow the man's words. But then the crisp figures of the sculptor began to come alive beneath his fingertips. He moved his hands in slow circles to touch the bulging muscles, the concave flanks. His fingers traveled over the crevices describing water, the ridges outlining the mastiff's ribs; he rubbed the knotty coils of the lion's mane. And he remembered the satisfaction of creating life between his hands.

He turned to Naboushoumidin. His breath was coming quicker now. Could it be possible that . . . ?

The man threw back his head and tossed forth a deep laugh that boomed across the vacant courtyard. When his eyes met Soulai's, they fairly crackled with animation. "Battles always bring new stories, and so we are beginning a new series of panels on the library's eastern wall tomorrow morning," he said. He glanced at the bag dangling from Soulai's hand. "You have choices."

By high sun on the same day as Habasle and Ti rode off to war, a messenger was dispatched to a mountain village carrying a bag of silver. Soulai was seated in the shade of a makeshift canopy that stretched along the eastern side of the library. Under the watchful eyes of a master craftsman, he was carefully chalking out the lines of the panel's first scene: a full-moon night when the king and his son announced impending victory for Assyria. Between them reared a brave, parti-color stallion, mane waving in the wind. Lovingly, Soulai sketched the broad forehead, the flared nostrils. A solid sense of worth filled him; he had found a new home. And whatever Ti's fate might be, he, Soulai, would make sure the horse was remembered forever.